GHOST MEADOW

GHOST MEADOW

by

Lauran Paine

The Golden West Large Print Books
Long Preston, North Yorkshire,
BD23 4ND, England.

British Library Cataloguing in Publication Data.

Paine, Lauran
    Ghost meadow.

    A catalogue record of this book is
    available from the British Library

    ISBN   978-1-84262-941-3 pbk

Published in Large Print 2013 by arrangement with
Golden West Literary Agency

The Golden West Large Print is an imprint of Library Magna
Books Ltd.

Printed and bound in Great Britain by
T.J. (International) Ltd., Cornwall, PL28 8R

I

He was the color of summer dust and had black eyes with hair to match, and, although it was customary among his kind to wear braids, John Morning Gun, who had spent two-thirds of his life among whites, reflected his inner ambiguity by wearing his hair fairly short, except for a thick length in back that he did not braid, but instead wore straight, with an animal vertebra holding it tightly in place. Morning Gun was tall and spare. He was also quick, observant, and given to long silences. In the *rancherías* he was known as a white Indian, and around Fort Laramie, where he was employed as a government hunter, he was known as 'different,' which was interpreted in half a dozen ways depending upon who used the term in connection with Morning Gun, and the degree of their prejudice, of which there was enough to go around.

He sat on the little shaded porch in the adjutant's hutment waiting for the conference inside to end, and during that time he watched troops cuffing mounts, hauling armloads of laundry to the wash house, and sweating in the midday summer heat while forking a load of timothy hay off a four-wheeled rack into the hay barn.

Inside the palisade, Fort Laramie was an insular world. Outside, particularly over at the town, not only were the people different, but the way they lived also was; civilians had little discipline. John Morning Gun knew about discipline. After the death of his mother – four days after he had been born – his father had loaded her body onto a horse, packed his possessions, and rode into the mountains never to return. The missionaries at their little log compound had taken in John. Now, thirty years later, he knew about discipline, first from the missionaries, then from his first and only employer, so far anyway, the U.S. Army.

Morning Gun was not a full-blood. In fact, it had not been his father who had been Indian, but his mother. His father had been one of those ubiquitous French-Canadian *voyageurs* who looked Indian, were not Indian, and acted more Indian than full-bloods acted. His dead wife, the Crow woman, had been called Snow Blossom. But in coloring Morning Gun looked full-blood. Most people assumed that he was, and because he did not discuss his personal background, or anything else personal, no one refuted the allegation that he was a full-blood.

Morning Gun's value to the Army lay not entirely in his ability as a hunter, tracker, horse wrangler, or non-drinking scout. It was in his ability to speak English with almost no accent, and in fact speak it more grammatically than nearly all the enlisted personnel at the fort, and many of the officers. Morning Gun's mother had been a Crow. Crows were for some obscure reason disliked and held in contempt by all their neighbors, including the Northern Cheyennes and the Sioux. But if a man was tall as the Sioux, shrewd and observant like the Cheyennes, and dressed in the motley manner of settlement tomahawks, and spoke very little Crow, or Cheyenne, or Sioux for that matter, and was fluent in English, did not wear a Crow roach or Sioux braids, then the tribesman who could not classify him properly simply said he was either a settlement Indian or an Army Indian. Even his name gave no clue, and, anyway, on the paymaster's records that was also incorrect.

He had been born shortly before noon on a bitterly cold February day thirty years earlier, in his father's hide tent that had been pitched as close to the fort's log walls as the Army would permit. It was common for Indians to name children for whatever first impressed their mothers after giving birth. It was also commonplace back in those days for the opening of the fort's log gates to be accompanied by the firing of a cannon.

It was always assumed that cannon shot

had been what had induced John's mother to give him his name. If anyone had bothered to look into the matter, they would have discovered that morning guns were fired as the big log gates were opened, usually about 6:00 in the morning, and John Morning Gun had not made his appearance in the world until after 11:00. The gun his mother had heard had been fired in honor of a trooper who had died a day or so earlier, and who had been buried that close to midday. It had not been the morning gun, it had been a mourning gun. If having his name arbitrarily altered had not bothered General Ulysses S. Grant, why should it bother John Morning Gun? It didn't. As nearly as those who knew John best could discern, very few things bothered Morning Gun. Not even the expressions of contempt he encountered occasionally among the soldiers. Or, if that and other things bothered him, it never showed.

He was, as Sergeant Flannery said, a dependable, decent Indian. Sergeant Michael Flannery was not only ham-fisted, red-faced, orange-haired, and pugnacious, given to drinking too much once he got started, but he was also big, raw-boned, and most important of all he had been in charge of latrine details around the fort for three years. No trooper argued with Mike Flannery unless he enjoyed such things as digging in hardpan, emptying slop buckets every day, and flies. If one of the periodic epidemics of dysentery arrived, the latrine details worked through days of unimaginable horror.

Morning Gun had another friend. His name was Lieutenant Albert Winthrop. He had been posted to the fort directly after graduation from the U.S. Military Academy on the Hudson River. Lieutenant Winthrop knew nothing about Indians. He knew even less about the West. His father had been successively a governor back East and a senator. Albert Winthrop had grown up remarkably free of prejudice, except against Democrats. He had been in Wyoming Territory thirteen months, and was reluctantly, sadly forming a prejudice. Not against Indians or the preponderantly treacherous civilians in his area, but against the Army. He had grown up with stars in his eyes. Thirteen months in Wyoming had been the greatest disillusionment of his life. But Lieutenant Winthrop was young, seven years younger than Morning Gun, and had such a fresh, clear, unmarred complexion that he looked much younger. It was unlikely, as demoralizing as this disillusionment was, that before the end of his life he would not encounter others just as demoralizing. But right now, as he and Sergeant Flannery stated their case before the post commander and his adjutant, Lieutenant Winthrop could read the adverse decision on the face of the two superior officers even before the seated captain leaned forward on the desk and said quietly: 'To my knowledge, Lieutenant, this has not happened before. That it has happened during my tour as commanding officer requires that I take the proper steps to correct it... Lieutenant, I know that you and Sergeant Flannery have faith in Morning Gun. So

13

have I. But the word of one Indian against the word of almost a dozen other people who saw those cattle being cut out and driven toward the mountains by Indians...' The officer leaned back in his chair. 'Lieutenant, what did you expect an Indian to say? I want you and Sergeant Flannery to take a detail and look for those cattle. I don't want you to take Morning Gun as scout and tracker. Take...' The captain turned toward his tall, blank-faced adjutant. 'What's his name, George?'

'Pierre Burdette. They call him Pete, sir.'

'That's your answer, Lieutenant. Take Burdette. And, Lieutenant, be very careful. You know by now it's not just the Indians, don't you?'

'Yes, sir.'

The captain said: 'Dismissed!'

The outside orderly, at his table in the small outer room, raised his eyes only after the sergeant and lieutenant had passed through to the yonder porch. Sunlight bounced back toward the orderly's open front door. He squinted and leaned to hear the lieutenant mutter something, and to watch the tall Indian arise to follow the other two men down across the parade ground in the direction of the horse area. When the tall adjutant strolled from his inner office into the orderly room, and looked down, the enlisted man gently wagged his head, then turned back to his paperwork.

Flannery perched his strong, lean body upon an empty wooden horseshoe keg and watched the boyish-looking officer. Morning Gun leaned nearby in impassive silence. He had been on the post a long time; he could have told the young officer it would be useless, maybe even damaging, for him to brace the captain. Winthrop looked older and tired as he stood in the shadow of a wash-rack overhang gazing out across the mustering area. He did not repeat what the captain had said about the Indian but simply said: 'You're to stay on the post, John. The sergeant and I are to take a detail and go after them.'

At Morning Gun's steady gaze toward the

office, Flannery added the rest of it: 'And take Pete Burdette.'

Now Morning Gun's gaze moved from Winthrop to Michael Flannery. He said nothing.

Flannery addressed the lieutenant. 'He'll lie when the truth will fit better, Lieutenant. I've been on patrols and scouts with him many times. And there's something else.'

Winthrop turned slightly to face the sergeant.

'Pete and that drover who brought in the beef allotment pee through the same knothole.'

Winthrop's brows dropped a notch as he gazed at the older man. He thought he understood but was not quite sure he did.

Flannery spoke more plainly: 'Burdette and that drover drink together in town. I've seen Pete ride out to the drover's camp night after night.'

The officer was still faintly scowling at the sergeant. Flannery shot a mildly exasperated glance at Morning Gun, then stood up off the little keg. 'Lieutenant, I know this is a hell of a thing to tell you. The captain was wrong. This ain't the first time cattle have disappeared from out there at the holding ground. Not only since he's been here, but before he came out here, too.'

Lieutenant Winthrop's stare hardened on the sergeant. He had become disillusioned with the Army, but for some reason he did not like to hear a non-commissioned officer make the kind of statement Flannery had just made. He said: 'Make up the detail. We'll leave first thing in the morning.'

Flannery reddened a little and nodded his head, then turned to watch the officer walk out into the sunlight on his way to his quarters. Behind him Morning Gun said: 'You scared him. What you said sounded like it wasn't just Indians or thieves who got away with those cattle.'

Flannery made a gesture of futility with his arms and sank back down upon the little wooden keg. 'The trouble is, John, a man could get real old on this post waiting for

17

someone to come out here who don't get scairt. Jesus! I know what I'm talking about. Do you expect they got corruption like this back in Washington?'

Morning Gun grinned in the shadows of the overhang. 'President Grant's brother stole allotment beef and re-sold it. Remember the scandal?'

Flannery sounded doleful when he replied: 'They never should have taught you to read, John.'

Morning Gun's grin lingered. 'Indians haven't believed you people are gods for hundreds of years. Mike, some of those cattle that've been siphoned off in the dark didn't end up in white stew pots. Indians've stolen their share.'

Flannery shrugged that off. 'That's not the point I wanted to make. But you've got to be careful what you say to officers. I wanted to tell him that the drovers who deliver the herds up here ain't the real thieves. That captain said no cattle had been stole until he showed up to take command. You know what that means, John? It means that someone who is supposed to keep the tallies and the books, and make sure the drovers get paid according to the number of cattle they're to deliver on a government contract are certifying that all the cattle have been delivered, and he's got to know damned well that they haven't all been turned over to us. What happened this time was simply that the fellers who drove off the cattle took too many and were too careless about how they did it. That's all it means. Hell, every herd that comes up here is shy the full number. You know that as well as I do, John. As well as someone else has to, by God, because he lies in the papers he makes out approving payment for the drover.'

Morning Gun said: 'Who?'

Flannery arose irritably and looked out across the compound. 'I'm just a non-com. I don't know anything. I'm not supposed to know anything.'

II

The result of the post adjutant's inquiries had indicated that the beef thieves had driven the cattle almost due west from Laramie, then southward where the land opened up into a wide, long trough of land down toward Colorado. The boundary between Wyoming and Colorado was not very far down in that direction. As the detachment rode through a blustery, alternately warm and cold springtime day, Lieutenant Winthrop, wrapped in his campaign coat and with his hat pulled down, gazed off on his right toward the mountains. They had eyewitness sightings, and some old, unreliable tracks to indicate the thieves had gone southward. Albert Winthrop may have lacked experience with Indian raiders, but over the last thirteen months he had learned a lot from listening.

Now he gazed dead ahead where the thick short man on the big-rumped, seal-brown horse was plodding along, his incongruous small-brimmed city hat sticking up above the moth-eaten massiveness of an old knee-length buffalo coat. Burdette had been around a long time. Longer than any of them, not just in years but in Wyoming Territory.

He was following those unidentifiable tracks as though he were certain they had been made by the missing cattle. What nagged at Lieutenant Winthrop were the stories he had heard about Indians avoiding areas like this which had roads traversing them. With stolen cattle – any cattle at all for that matter – Indians would not pass openly in country like this. He told himself the tracks would turn westerly soon; the thieves would leave open country for the mountains. But when the detail of twelve men stopped in the lee of a sandstone shelter to rest the animals and Burdette came back where the officer was standing, smiling to show three gold teeth, with his little dark eyes fixed upon Winthrop, he gestured with a mittened hand and said: 'They had a hell of a start on us. But I expect if we was to push right along, we might be able to come onto something. Cattle can't be drove hard, like horses can, Lieutenant.'

Winthrop gazed at the shorter, older, and darker man. 'You think they continued southward?'

Burdette's smile broadened. 'I expect so. Unless we find that they turned off down-country somewhere.'

'This is open country, Mister Burdette.'

The scout understood Winthrop's implication. 'Well, sir, if they come down through here in the night … which I'd have done in their boots just exactly because it is open country, they wouldn't lose no cattle, would they, like they'd sure as hell do if they taken them into the hills?'

Winthrop did not press this conversation. He watched the troopers at work on their meager rations, and eventually strolled over

23

where Sergeant Flannery was examining one of the hoofs of his horse. He said: 'Anything wrong?'

Flannery straightened up, wiping his hands. 'You mean with my horse, sir?'

Winthrop stood gazing at the raw-boned man with the green eyes. 'What else would I mean?'

Flannery's bold gaze crinkled with sardonic humor. 'You might mean, sir, that we're never going to find those cattle.'

'Why, Sergeant?'

'Because there's lots of cattle down through this slot. There's ranchers on both sides of the stage road, and they got free-ranging cattle all around through here, and we're not following fresh tracks. Most of all, Lieutenant, we're not following barefoot horses.'

Winthrop shoved cold hands deeper into his coat pockets and let his gaze drift back where Pete Burdette and some enlisted men were talking.

Sergeant Flannery watched the officer for a moment, then spoke again. 'Being an officer gives a man a chance to speak his mind, Lieutenant.'

Winthrop showed irritation. 'What you'd like to say is that someone on the post besides the drover helped someone steal the cattle, isn't that it?'

Michael Flannery's smile faded as he returned the officer's troubled gaze. 'Lieutenant, there's a lot I'd like to say. I've been out here a long time. Right now, what I'd like to say is that Pete Burdette is getting our tails froze off for nothing. We're not going to find those cattle, and we're not going to find Indians driving them. I thought you believed what John said when we went out to the holding ground day before yesterday. Hell, Lieutenant, you stood up to the captain about that. It wasn't Indians.'

Lieutenant Winthrop gazed moodily southward. He had not only stated his belief, based upon Morning Gun's judgment, that Indians had not stolen the cattle, but he could have added something to it right now. He did not like Pete Burdette, or trust the man. Instead of mentioning these things, he brought his gaze back to the raw-boned Irishman. 'The problem as I see it, Sergeant, is whether or not Burdette is taking us on a wild-goose chase. Each day that passes we're losing more chances of ever finding those cattle.'

Flannery agreed instantly. 'Yes, sir, an' that's what I meant a minute ago. Burdette's doin' this on purpose.'

Winthrop's gaze hardened a little. 'Pete Burdette…?'

Flannery did not falter. 'Why not, Lieutenant? Him and most of those drovers are as close as peas in a pod.'

Winthrop looked over where the man in the old buffalo coat was swinging his arms in the cold, still talking with the enlisted men. 'You can't just guess about things like this, Sergeant.'

Flannery's wide, thin mouth pulled up at the corners. 'Lieutenant, if they'd've let us bring John along, we maybe would be riding in a different direction.'

For a while Winthrop stood in silent

thought, then, as he was turning away, he said: 'But they didn't... I agree with you about one thing. Morning Gun would be more helpful than Burdette is.'

Flannery watched the officer go to his horse, catch the tracker's eye, and jerk his head. When they were astride again, still heading southward, Flannery delved inside his coat for a plug, tore off a corner, pouched the cud, returned the plug to an inner pocket, then leaned and lustily expectorated. Afterward he rode along, studying the man out in front in the old buffalo coat.

The wind increased. They were passing down through a broad slot with mountains on both sides. Any ground-hugging wind in this kind of country was compressed between mountains and with only one funnel to flow through, of necessity had to become pro-longed and fierce. If there could be a saving grace to something like this, it had to be that both horses and men had their backs to the wind. But wind in the Laramie plains coun-try was endowed with a capacity for cutting through the thickest clothing. It was not the cold that increased Sergeant Flannery's irritability, as much as it was his solid conviction that they were making this long, forced ride with no prospect of accomplishing anything, and they still had to ride back, *facing* the damned wind when they turned northward.

Two hours later, when Burdette led them aside into a spit of pine and fir trees that served as a windbreak, Flannery got down with the others, and sprang his knees a few times to get some of the cold-induced stiffness out. When a bull-necked, leathery-faced trooper spoke from nearby, saying unprintable things about springtime in Wyoming, Flannery nodded absently while watching the lieutenant and the tracker in conversation up ahead. He spat, rubbed his hands together, then tucked each one under an armpit. His irritability had progressed through indignation to anger. Burdette was making a monkey out of the lieutenant, which, as a non-commissioned officer, Flannery normally would not have objected to, except that this particular officer did not go around with a damned ramrod up his back. Also, what Sergeant Flannery considered as Burdette's underhanded duplicity was responsible for the suffering among the detail, which included himself.

Flannery had been a solider for a long time. He had seen things that angered him, but after so many years, while he never learned to accept stupidity, dishonesty, and pomposity with grace, he had just about become fatalistic about it. Then Winthrop had come along, and what that damned tracker was doing right now amounted to the deliberate discrediting of a green officer, who happened to possess the virtues Sergeant Flannery had once had, and still had but not in the same degree as the lieutenant had. He knew from watching Winthrop that disillusionment was setting in. He also knew from years of experience with other officers as fresh and idealistic as Winthrop was, that when it got bad enough, they either quit the Army, or they turned to whiskey.

Flannery swung his arms and saw the tracker and the lieutenant break off their discussion and head for their animals. Flannery turned and growled at the detail, and, as he, too, swung across the McClellan and evened up the reins, he watched Burdette from narrowed eyes. They would not be able to get back to the post today, and, although they were equipped to spend the night out, it was not going to be a pleasant bivouac.

Unpleasant overnight camps were nothing new to Sergeant Flannery. Since being posted to Wyoming Territory he had rarely survived any other kind, and normally, on patrol or reconnaissance in the past, he had accepted the discomfort with soldierly fatalism, but this time he knew as well as he knew his name that the lieutenant, and all of them for that matter, were being made fools of, and that made a difference as he plodded along, watching Burdette with his green eyes in slits. Sleeping like cocoons on half-frozen ground was bad enough, doing it because the scout was being crafty made it worse. But

Flannery kept his anger inside. When they eventually arrived down where there were more trees to break the bitter wind and swung off to make camp, Flannery got as busy as the other enlisted men organizing the camp. When Lieutenant Winthrop came over where the men had a whip-sawing fire going and hunkered down near the sergeant, Flannery deliberately smiled as he said: 'How much farther south does he aim to go?'

Winthrop gathered his coat close and leaned toward heat when he replied: 'No farther. We'll turn back in the morning.'

'No more tracks to follow, Lieutenant?'

'He didn't say that. He said they've been making better time and widening the gap, and, unless we're prepared to spend two weeks in the field, we'd better just go back.'

Flannery turned toward the fire and held out both palms. His smile was gone; there was a high flush in his face, and he had no more to say.

The lieutenant went after his blanket roll. One of the squatting enlisted men waited until Winthrop was beyond hearing, then said: 'That's what the Army is all about. Ride out, ride back, get in line to wait, freeze your tail off … or damn' near die of thirst in summer time … and put in the time until your enlistment is up.'

That bull-necked man with the leathery face pushed closer to the blaze. 'What did you think it was, bein' a hero?'

The discussion lagged for want of other participants. Flannery looked for Burdette. He had his own little fire in a secluded area with trees on three sides. He was cooking something, was smoking a little pipe, and on the ground in that thick old coat with patches of hair worn off put Flannery in mind of an old bear with mange.

A tall, gaunt soldier, following the sergeant's stare, said: 'You fellers remember Sergeant Evinrude? He was invalided out with a ruined back about six years ago. One time him and me was in Laramie having a few drinks, and he told me something about Pete Burdette, said Burdette used to trap and pot-hunt for the settlements back in the early days. Said he lived with the Indians for some years, and got into trouble once when the Army found a bunch of their horses in some Indian camp where Pete was living.'

Flannery had never heard this tale, although he had heard others about their scout. 'How did he get out of it?'

'Evinrude said he swore up an' down the Indians had stolen them horses and that he hadn't known a danged thing about it.' The tall, lean man shook his head. 'The patrol fetched back some of the Indians, and Burdette taken off for higher into the mountains and didn't come back for several years.'

A soldier waited, then said: 'That's all?'

The gaunt man nodded his head.

Flannery finally had enough heat penetrating his clothing to relax his muscles. He saw Burdette arise from his cooking fire and head back through the trees. For a while Flannery remained in place, then he casually arose and walked out into the settling cold and blustery darkness. No one paid much attention.

There was a little moon that cast almost no light, and a million stars that cast slightly more light, but among the trees visibility was about as it would have been if there had been no stars, so Flannery had to pick his way carefully. He particularly did not want to make a lot of noise.

When he passed Pete Burdette's little untended fire, he did so well to the north so he could not be outlined by it. Back where the men were sitting, someone suddenly laughed loudly; evidently the heat was relaxing everyone a little. Flannery halted until the noise of laughter ended, then listened. But the wind made many different kinds of sound as it beat through tree limbs and against the congealing earth, so he continued his scout relying almost entirely upon his eyes.

He found Burdette by accident, as the shorter and thicker man came forth from a thorn-pin thicket and struck a match to rekindle his little pipe. Wind whipped the flame out almost immediately but not before Burdette had sucked twice, fast, to get the shag burning again. Flannery waited beside a tree until Burdette started past in the direction of his camp, then stepped out to block the scout's progress.

Burdette recoiled, his right hand dipping to brush back the coat. Flannery's teeth flashed in the gloom. Burdette recognized him and let go with smoke and profanity at the same time. 'You like to scairt the hell out of me!' he exclaimed.

Flannery stepped a little closer, still smiling.

III

They were a mismatched pair, like a horse in harness with a burro. Flannery was tall and lean, Burdette was shorter, thick and solid. The bear-skin coat made him look much thicker. Flannery was a career non-commissioned soldier who was unaccustomed to tact – unless he was speaking to an officer. Scouts and Army hunters were not in the officer category. In fact, on most posts they weren't considered even to be in the class of private soldiers. Flannery said: 'Pete, those are old tracks we been following.'

Burdette removed his little pipe, spat, plugged the pipe back between his teeth, and steadily eyed the sergeant. 'Whose fault is that?' he eventually asked.

Flannery was not to be diverted. He said: 'This whole country down here's got cattle through it. And there ain't been any bare-foot horse tracks.'

Burdette did as he had done before, he stared at the larger man and sucked on his pipe before eventually speaking. 'I'm the scout, Flannery, you ain't. Indians don't have to ride barefoot horses. I've seen 'em riding shod horses and so have you.' Burdette cocked his head a little. 'What are you gettin' at … and, remember, the lieutenant's goin' to hear about this?'

Flannery's deep-down indignation rose up a notch. 'Is that supposed to scare me, Pete?'

'No. It's supposed to make you think before you get to runnin' off at the mouth. Sergeant, we never been friends, and that's all right with me. But you want to be a mite careful.'

Flannery considered the older man. When he spoke, his voice was tinged with irony. 'You're goin' to tell me you got the captain's ear. I figured you'd be too smart to threaten me.'

'I ain't threatenin' no one, Sergeant. I know how many times you been in fights and all. I know your reputation. I don't want no trouble with you if I can avoid it.'

Flannery bobbed his head. 'Good. Then tell me straight out why you brought us down here when you know damned well those stolen cattle didn't go south at all?'

Again the scout puffed and eyed Flannery with his head to one side. 'They didn't go south? Then which direction did they go in?'

Flannery did not know so he said: 'Not south. So what you're goin' to tell me right here and now is why you been tellin' the lieutenant we're following their marks?'

Burdette removed the pipe and knocked out the dottle on the palm of a gloved hand. He was pensive when he eventually looked up again. 'Flannery, you are tryin' to make trouble. I know how you do this, I been on the post as long as you have. You keep this up, and when we get back to the fort I'm goin' to the captain. We *are* followin' their tracks!'

'You're lying, Pete. We both know it and I want to know why you're lying.'

Burdette stowed his little pipe somewhere inside the old coat, and afterward pushed back the coat on both sides with his hands on his hips. He showed no fear at all of the taller and younger man. He carried one of the late-model Colt six-shooters, a better, more advanced sidearm than the Army had issued to its non-coms and officers.

'Sergeant, the officer believes me. That's what matters. Not what some non-commissioned lifer believes. Sergeant, you make trouble right now and I'll shoot you.'

Flannery had his sidearm, but made no move toward it. He instead smiled at the older man, ignoring the threat. 'It wasn't Indians, Pete. You know that it wasn't. And they didn't come down through here. If you want to report me when we get back, you go right ahead.'

Burdette picked out just one of those statements. 'Wasn't Indians, then who was it?'

'White men.'

'You're crazy, Flannery.'

'White men this time and other times, too.

You and the drovers know that. Pete, I've watched you take details out like this over the years, an' you never brought back no cattle nor no cattle thieves.'

Flannery let it lie between them without putting it into words, confident that Burdette knew exactly what he was implying.

Burdette understood. He said: 'Flannery, you'd better have something more than Irish blarney to back that up. You called me a liar, and now you're sayin' I'm helpin' rustle cattle.'

The taller man looked down. They were no more than ten feet apart, much too close for the scout to get his gun out before Flannery rushed him. 'Who was it this time, Pete?' he asked quietly.

Burdette's weathered, tan face looked much darker in the night; if there was red in it, that was not noticeable, but the expression was readable. He was coldly furious and calculatingly silent. For a long time he returned the sergeant's stare before speaking again. 'I'll give you a warnin',' he said. 'Don't

41

stick your nose where it's got no business.'

Flannery was not intimidated. 'That's no warning, Pete. That's admittin' something. You want to tell me who stole those cattle now? You're not goin' to get a chance to use that gun before I beat your damned brains out, if you don't.'

A sharp, angry voice cut in from behind Flannery. 'Sergeant! What the hell do you think you're doing?'

Lieutenant Winthrop walked stiffly around in front of Flannery, his eyes narrowed in anger, his shoulders squared and both gloved hands fisted at his side. They exchanged a wintry long look before the officer ordered Flannery to return to the bivouac for enlisted men.

Flannery stood his ground for a moment, then wheeled and stamped back the way he had come through the trees.

Lieutenant Winthrop faced Pete Burdette, still furious. If the scout expected some ameliorating words, he must have been surprised when the officer spoke to him. 'What did you mean that he shouldn't stick his nose where it didn't belong?'

Burdette shifted his feet a little before answering. 'I meant that he ain't the scout, I am. And I know my trade better'n any damned soldier knows it. That's what I meant, Lieutenant. I'm a civilian, I don't have to take no crap from any soldier.'

Winthrop regarded the scout for a moment before speaking again. 'It didn't sound to me like that's what you meant.'

'Well, Lieutenant, I can't help what it sounded like to you. That's exactly what I meant. He's mad because we been ridin' in bad weather for so long. Hell, I don't make the weather. And I been on plenty of scouts before where we come back empty-handed, and that ain't been my fault, either.'

Winthrop turned and walked back through the trees, leaving Pete Burdette to stand out there a long time, looking after Winthrop, his expression gradually turning crafty and hostile. When he eventually got back to his little fire, he had to go hunt up more dry twigs because there was nothing left but red embers.

The wind died sometime in the night, which was somewhat of a blessing, but when wind died on a cold night, the temperature plummeted, so shortly before dawn, when Sergeant Flannery routed out the detail, there was frozen earth underfoot, a condition that inevitably soured dispositions and sharpened the talent men had for profanity.

They struck camp in haste because the lieutenant wanted to reach the post before evening. Two miles on their way northward they encountered some packers coming in from the westerly mountains with a string of sixteen handsome big Missouri mules. While the lieutenant rode over to talk with the packers, Flannery and the other enlisted man squatted where thin sunshine fell across their backs. Burdette, as usual, did not go over among the soldiers, but hunkered by himself on the lee side of his horse, even though there was no wind blowing.

Two more hours northward, with Sergeant

Flannery maintaining at least some semblance of military order by riding a couple of yards ahead of the details, Lieutenant Albert Winthrop looked back and curtly beckoned. Flannery obediently gigged his mount. He had been looking at the lieutenant's back since they'd struck camp, wondering whether he'd got all the disciplining he was going to get last night, or whether the lieutenant would make formal charges when they got back to the post. An argument was hardly enough to warrant a complaint and disciplinary action, but a man could never be sure with officers, especially with one like Winthrop who was going through a bad time of disillusionment and frustration.

When he got up beside the officer, Winthrop faced him and said: 'Don't do anything like that again.'

Flannery nodded. The officer's remonstrance hadn't sounded even annoyed, and his attitude was not as it should have been when he was scolding an enlisted man.

'Those packers were returning empty

from the mines in the westerly mountains.'

Flannery nodded about that, also. Those packers didn't have any connection with him bracing Burdette, as far as Flannery could see.

Winthrop loosened his coat because as the day advanced the heat increased. It was turning out to be one of those magnificent springtime days with wildflowers along the way, a few drifting thin high clouds, and a brilliant sun.

'Those packers,' Winthrop said quietly, looking past Burdette who was about half a mile ahead, 'have been over quite a bit of country. Northward for a couple of weeks, then down through the mountains on our left. They didn't see any Indian camps, Sergeant.'

Flannery's suspicion stirred but he still said nothing because quite clearly Lieutenant Winthrop had more to say.

Winthrop turned his head slowly. 'Up north and according to the packers about fifty miles through the mountains at a series of gold diggings, while they were trading up there, some stockmen arrived in the meadows with a band of cattle.'

Flannery fished inside his coat for the plug of tobacco and worried off a cud. He spat, eyed the lieutenant with sardonic green eyes, and straightened up in the saddle. 'Ours,' he said. 'Except that the packers didn't know that.'

'And I didn't tell them, Sergeant, and you're not going to mention this to anyone.'

As though the admonition was not only uncalled for, but irritating, Flanner scowled at his officer and did not deign to offer assurance. Instead he said: 'The brand...?'

'The same, Sergeant. The previous owner's brand and his road brand.'

'Indians?'

'Of course not, Sergeant.'

Flannery spat aside again, eyes puckered in faint amusement. This was the same man who yesterday got his back up when Flannery had reiterated what Morning Gun had said about the rustlers not having been

Indians. Flannery took a sideswipe of his own, but he was careful in the way he did it. 'And here we are, down where those stolen cattle never come.'

Winthrop reddened a little and slouched along a short distance in silence before saying: 'I've been thinking, Sergeant. We're going to keep this between us, and, when we get back to the post, I'm going to get Morning Gun to ask for leave, then go up into that northwesterly country and find at least one of the hides off those cattle the miners butchered, and fetch it back to the post.'

'With the brand on it.'

'Naturally,' replied the officer, watching Burdette up ahead. The scout had finally shed his mangy old riding coat and was riding, twisted from the waist, while he tied the coat behind his cantle. 'Sergeant, stay away from Burdette.'

Flannery was perfectly agreeable. 'Yes, sir. That suits me fine. Suppose he goes and complains to his friend, the adjutant, that I called him a liar?'

48

'I'll handle that,' stated Winthrop with full confidence that he would be able to. 'By any chance do you know the drover who brought in that last herd of cattle?'

'No, sir. I know a few of them, but not that one.'

'Too bad,' muttered the lieutenant.

Flannery knew what the lieutenant had in mind, but as far as he knew there was no one on the post, except Pete Burdette, who knew the stockman. His thoughts reverted to the packers. 'Did you get the names of those traders?'

Winthrop had. 'Yes. They make up their packs of trading goods down around Fort Collins in Colorado, but they trade up through the gold diggings of southern and western Wyoming. They'll be back through in a couple of months. I got an address down in Fort Collins where they can be reached.' As the officer finished speaking, he gazed at Flannery. 'They also gave me some other names.'

Flannery smiled a little. 'Descriptions

would most likely be better, Lieutenant. Rustlers change names oftener you an' me change shirts.'

'I have their descriptions, too,' stated Winthrop, looking ahead again. 'But what they couldn't provide me with was anything about someone around the post who helped those men steal the cattle, so I didn't ask. But I need to know that.'

Flannery nodded his head. 'They wouldn't have known, if they just bumped into the rustlers. Anyway, if you hadn't gone and got your hackles up last night, I'd have got that information out of Pete.'

Winthrop slowly wagged his head. 'If you had, you'd have spilled the beans, Flannery. If Burdette is part of it, which I don't know is the case, but if he is, and you'd kicked the wadding out of him to get answers, what do you think he'd do the minute he got back to Laramie?'

Flannery avoided an incriminating, and embarrassing, answer by saying: 'I'd kind of like to make that ride into the mountains with John. This is the most beautiful time of the year for...'

'You are going to stay on the post, Sergeant. Morning Gun can make it better without you along, and I've got something in mind.'

Flannery rode along in silence for a long time, feeling much better than he had felt yesterday. He could even smile at Burdette's back half a mile up ahead.

IV

They made it before the evening meal, but without enough time left to do much more than care for their animals, and afterward, when Lieutenant Winthrop presented himself to the adjutant's hutment to report, he was told by the orderly that the captain and adjutant had ridden down to the town and would not be back until only God knew when. It was the same steady-eyed, stone-faced orderly who had seen Winthrop and Flannery storm out of the adjutant's office after their meeting with the captain, and this time, as he watched Lieutenant Winthrop depart, his lips pulled back in a humorless smile.

Flannery was out back leaning on a corral, chewing and talking to John Morning Gun when the lieutenant made a round that took him back there. The other two stopped talking when he came up, which irritated him, but he simply hooked a boot over the lowest rail and told Morning Gun what he wanted him to do in the morning – ask for leave for a week or two, find one of those hides with a brand on it, and bring it back.

John Morning Gun thought about that for a while before agreeing. Then he walked away, leaving the sergeant and lieutenant alone. For Morning Gun the decision had not been difficult; the reason he was slow to assent was because his mind was full of the things Flannery had told him about their ride southward. He had been convinced from their first brief little cursory scout after the cattle had been stolen that the thieves had not been Indians. Until the detail had returned, though, he had gloomily considered anyone's chances of proving it just about impossible, because something he had noticed at other times seemed to be working. The willingness of the Army to believe reservation jumpers were at the bottom of everything bad that happened.

After he walked away, Sergeant Flannery mused aloud to the lieutenant: 'Suppose they won't let him go?'

Winthrop answered shortly. 'He's a civilian. They can't prevent it.'

'They can fire him off the post.'

'They won't do that,' stated the lieutenant.

Flannery shrugged. He would know tomorrow whether they could prevent it or not; meanwhile he had something else on his mind. 'I saw Pete come out of the adjutant's hut a while ago.'

Lieutenant Winthrop said nothing. He was watching the horses in the corral. They had been fed and were lipping up the few remaining stalks they could find.

Flannery decided to risk the lieutenant's anger and said: 'The adjutant's orderly, Corporal Krause, sat in there for more'n an hour with Burdette.'

Still the officer watched the horse, his face reflecting somber thoughts while he remained silent.

Flannery's patience was slipping a little. 'Lieutenant, I can talk to Krause.'

Finally Winthrop spoke. 'Like you were going to do with Burdette? Sergeant, you'll end up in the stockade, and, if anyone in uniform is involved, your action will simply let them know you suspect something. Just be patient. I know it's hard, but it'll be worse if we start accusing people with nothing to go on. We'll do nothing until Morning Gun returns.'

Flannery, too, faced ahead to watch the horses. In his mind there was a question. *Suppose Morning Gun returns without a hide?* But he said nothing.

Lieutenant Winthrop strolled away, heading for the officers' hutments, and Flannery got a fresh chew of molasses-cured tobacco in his cheek and wandered over to the latrine area to make sure the detail was at work. It was; at least the men were busy when Flannery arrived, so he headed toward the barracks.

That leather-faced, bull-necked trooper

who had been with the detail was sitting out front, whittling in very poor light. He snapped his Barlow closed and pocketed it as the sergeant walked up. With his eyes on Flannery he said: 'Mike, there's something *underhanded* going on, isn't there?'

Flannery looked down, then turned to expectorate before answering. 'Otto, you been soldierin' as long as I have, so you know there's always something goin' on at a post.'

The trooper tossed his whittled stick out into the yard. 'I said something underhanded, Mike.'

Flannery chewed, then dragged an old chair around, sat on it, and leaned back against the log wall before speaking again. 'What makes you think that?' he asked, and got a withering look from the barrel-built man at his side.

'You're playing games, Mike. That ain't like you.'

'Well, damn it, Otto, talkin' like you're doin' isn't like you.'

The bull-necked man stood up. 'Keep your

god-damned secret,' he said, and entered the building.

Flannery sighed, enjoyed his cud, and, when the detail went out to the flagstaff, the bugler with his instrument tucked under his arm, Flannery sighed, jettisoned his cud, and also went inside.

A large red-necked replacement whose uniform was still unfaded was telling several other replacements that the only way enlisted men could assert their rights to better meals and a larger soap allotment was to stand up for themselves. Sergeant Flannery heard part of this pronouncement as he entered the barracks, and halted back near the door gazing at the broad back of the red-necked newcomer. Nearby, seated on his bunk, Otto Burck, the man who had indignantly left Flannery alone on the porch moments earlier, was gazing at the big red-necked recruit with an expression of malicious amusement. He and the men facing the recruit saw Sergeant Flannery back by the door, but the rabble-rouser did not because his back was to the door.

He balled a big fist and struck the palm of his other hand with it. 'It's workin' back East. Fellers who work in them sweatshop factories banded together and stopped the wheels from turning. That's where the strength of the workin' people lies. Standin' together!'

Otto Burck spoke from his seat on a nearby bunk. 'What's your name?' he asked the big recruit, and got a truculent reply.

'You ought to know what it is. I been here two weeks now. It's Arthur Anderson, and your name is Otto Burck, and...'

'And,' said a flat voice from the doorway, 'my name is Sergeant Michael Patrick Flannery.'

The big recruit turned. The men he had been addressing began to move off, toward their own bunk areas. The replacement stood his ground. Flannery was no taller than he was, and there was a considerable age and weight difference between them, in favor of the big recruit.

Flannery strolled ahead. 'I guess they

forgot to tell you in trainin', Private Anderson, but talkin' like you was doing is called incitin' to mutiny. It is punishable by death before a firin' squad.' Flannery halted directly in front of the younger and heavier man, and he smiled directly into the other man's face. 'Most places I been, though, we don't make a lot of paperwork, we try to keep things inside the walls of the barracks. It works better that way.'

He hit Private Anderson a rapier-blow, at the very last moment twisting all his body weight in behind the fist. Anderson's legs did not even bend. He reached and with both hands caught Sergeant Flannery by the blouse, and lifted him three inches off the floor, then flung him backward. Flannery went across to a large old barracks table, which went over with him to the floor. The noise of men scattering in all directions followed the crash of the big table.

Flannery rolled once and came up to his feet. The big recruit hadn't moved. From his nearby bunk Otto Burck spoke to the recruit

– 'Bread and water for thirty days, Anderson.' – and arose to walk flat-footedly toward the larger man. He was wearing a crooked, humorless little smile. The younger man turned slowly, both arms at his sides. He was big enough and strong enough; he was also full of confidence. Otto halted just beyond reach and shook his head. 'Why in hell do we always have to get one like you when they send the replacements?' He moved like a crab, to one side, then farther around until the big recruit had to shift position, which was what Otto expected. While the recruit was shuffling his feet, Otto went in low.

Anderson's thick arms came up, hands clubbed for battle. Flannery swore at Otto: 'Damn it, keep out of this!'

Neither Burck nor any of the other men seemed to have heard. Otto straightened up to draw a strike. When it came, Otto went inside it and hit Anderson first in the middle, then over the heart, and finally, as the big man's arms were dropping, squarely in the face. Anderson's body wilted, his eyes were glazed. Otto straightened up, took the measurement, and dropped the larger man with one not particularly powerful blow alongside the head.

There was not a sound in the barracks. Sergeant Flannery blew out a big, noisy breath, and leaned to raise the table. Otto Burck turned toward the wide-eyed troopers and smiled. 'It don't go no farther than this room.' Then he went back to his bunk and Sergeant Flannery, red in the face, went over and stood, looking down.

A man across from Burck's bunk who had watched the entire affair lying flat out with both hands under his head said: 'He saved your bacon, Mike.' Several other of the old hands muttered agreement and Otto smiled up at Flannery, then looked around for the button and thread he'd been working on when the ruckus started.

Flannery turned on his heel, red as a beet, and walked back out into the chilly night. He was still out there when Burck came forth and, leaning on the nearest hitch rack, said:

'You could have done it maybe better'n I did, Mike. What that farm lad needed to learn was that this ain't back East, and on a post the old hands outnumber the greenhorns.'

Flannery turned. 'It wasn't your affair, Otto.'

Burck gazed with narrowed eyes around the large, dusty parade ground. 'I know. It seemed to me, him and the other replacements had to learn they're a minority. That's all I wanted to get across to them. I didn't mean to step on your toes.'

Flannery's indignation faded a little. After a moment he stepped closer to the porch and leaned there, shaking his head. 'That son-of-a-bitch is as strong as a bear.'

Otto chuckled. 'Yeah. While you was out with the detail, I been watchin' him. He's been talkin' like that since he arrived. It was goin' to happen, Mike, whether you came back in time or not.'

'I guess so. Well … all right. You most likely made a believer out of him.'

'Mike, about this underhanded business

that's goin' on…'

'Go to bed,' stated Flannery shortly, and went back inside, leaving Burck leaning out there, shaking his head.

The barracks was quiet when Flannery entered. The old hands were bedded down as though nothing had happened. The replacements were also bedding down, but probably for a different reason; they had something to think about. Private Anderson was in his blankets, his face to the wall. Flannery stopped briefly to watch him, then went on his way. He was tired, the day had begun early even by Army standards, the ride had been long, and most of all he had felt bitter about a number of things for several days.

The bugler trumpeted new life into the post in the predawn, and by the time daily details had been read off at first muster, Sergeant Flannery learned from one of the stable men that Morning Gun had left the post during the night. Later, when he was standing nearby watching Anderson and the other new men taking over the previous latrine detail, Otto passed by saying: 'Lieutenant Winthrop wants to see you at the corrals.'

Flannery went down there expecting to be told what he already knew, that John Morning Gun was gone. He was only partly correct. The lieutenant did indeed inform him of this fact, then he also said: 'Adjutant Fessler is going to brace you. Burdette complained.'

Flannery eyed the officer. 'Just brace me?'

Winthrop nodded. 'This time. Next time he's going to have you reduced in rank. He would have tried it this time but Burdette told him I witnessed your near attack on him. I told the adjutant Burdette was making a mountain out of a molehill, that we were all tired and discouraged.' Winthrop gazed around the horse area where men were working without noticeable enthusiasm or haste. 'Stay away from Pete.'

Flannery agreed. 'Yes, sir. Thanks for scotchin' it. The adjutant don't like me. He'll put this into his little black book.'

Lieutenant Winthrop said: 'Do you like

him, Mike?'

Flannery smiled broadly. 'No, sir, now that you mention it, I sure don't.'

'Then keep your big mouth closed when he bawls you out,' stated the younger man, and walked away.

Flannery laughed to himself and watched Lieutenant Winthrop cross in the direction of the mess hall.

Later, when the adjutant's pale-eyed, thin-lipped orderly came looking for Flannery, and told him that by order of post adjutant he was to return to the adjutant's office with him, Flannery was prepared. The adjutant was a large, handsome man who appeared as the ideal of what newsmen and others thought a frontier Army officer should be. And he worked at maintaining that image. He also worked at cultivating the post commander's confidence and friendship. Also, it was true that he did not like Sergeant Flannery. Whatever his reasons, he kept them to himself, but when his orderly, Corporal Krause, appeared stiffly in the office doorway to announce that Flannery was waiting, Lieutenant Fessler nodded, stood up to smooth his uniform. When Flannery entered and the orderly closed the door behind him, Lieutenant Fessler clasped both hands behind his back and stood like a large, blue statue, gazing steadily at the equally as tall but less handsome and elegant non-commissioned officer.

He finally spoke. 'I have a complaint against your conduct while on patrol with Lieutenant Winthrop's detail.'

Flannery was at attention, looking straight back. 'Yes, sir!'

'You threatened Mister Burdette.'

'Well ... yes, sir!'

The adjutant frowned. 'Did you or did you not threaten him, Sergeant?' Before Flannery could reply, the large officer unclasped his hands and leaned with them atop the desk, his eyes wide and angry. 'You don't say you're going to beat someone's brains out unless you are threatening them, Flannery.'

'Yes, sir ... I threatened him.'

The lieutenant continued to lean on the desk and glare. He straightened up slowly, and considered some papers atop his desk before speaking again, and now his voice reflected strong reluctance. 'This has been a warning, Sergeant. You've made trouble at other times. This will be your final warning. If you come up before me one more time, you'll be reduced to private rank.'

'Yes, sir.'

They looked steadily at each other for several seconds, then the adjutant made a curt gesture of dismissal, and turned his back. 'That's all. Dismissed!'

Flannery was careful to close the door after himself with care. His eyes met the gaze of Corporal Krause. The orderly had a hint of a very faint smile down around his lips.

For a moment Flannery stood near the orderly desk, looking down, then he abruptly left the building, went down off the little porch, and halted fifty feet out in the sunshine to look back before he continued on his way.

V

They had a patrol to ride the fourth day after the disappearance of Morning Gun, with the adjutant along. Because his commission was oldest he was technically the officer commanding, but because Lieutenant Winthrop was by the post commander's orders in charge of the patrol, Lieutenant Fessler rode along as an observer. There were several designations to fit this kind of situation. The adjutant invoked none of them; he was a discreet man when discretion was required. As he rode with Albert Winthrop, he was pleasant. Not quite unbending, but pleasant.

Lieutenant Winthrop, on the other hand, was reticent. He allowed himself to be drawn out only on general matters, such as the weather, the purpose of the patrol, and eventually, as their discussion continued, his

69

thoughts about an Army career. He told George Fessler that when his last two years were served he would leave the Army. The adjutant grew thoughtful after that, not commenting until they had a noon halt beside a cold-water creek that was literally hidden by willow thickets that ran north and south as far as the men could see. Then, while lying in the sunshine and shade, Lieutenant Fessler made a suggestion.

'You can request a transfer, Albert. You can put in for something east of the Missouri where there is civilized life and better accommodations.'

Winthrop ate and watched a high, stem-winding, red-tailed hawk cover more of the pale sky each time he widened his sweeps.

'The captain would approve a transfer for you,' stated the handsome adjutant. 'One thing that can be said in favour of Captain Brewster is that he understands things like this. He's transferred a number of officers since I've been out here.'

Winthrop turned narrowed eyes. 'You like

it out here, George?'

Fessler was brushing dead grass off his tunic when he replied: 'After four years I'm accustomed to it. I wouldn't say I like it, but then I don't quite dislike it, either.'

Winthrop searched the sky for the hawk, but its widening circles had carried it beyond sight from the ground by the creek. Winthrop changed the subject. 'How did Flannery take being reprimanded?'

Fessler stopped brushing off grass. He did not answer the question directly. 'Flannery is one of those wise old lifers. He has been in trouble of one kind or another ever since I've been here. He's been up before me before. It's infuriating to have one of those lifers stand at attention looking you straight in the eye, sneering at you without showing anything on their faces. Flannery isn't the only one, but he's the worst.' Anger had prodded George Fessler further than he would ordinarily have gone, so when he paused and saw Winthrop pluck a grass stalk and chew on it while looking stonily dead ahead, Fessler backtracked a little. 'I know he backed you on that story about white men having run of the cattle. I know you take him on details and patrols with you.'

Winthrop took the grass from his lips and squinted at it. 'He's experienced, George, I'm not.'

Fessler accepted that as an oblique apology for Winthrop's taking the sergeant with him, and felt better. He said: 'That damned Indian left the post almost a week go.'

Winthrop continued to gaze at the stalk of grass in his hand. 'You mean Morning Gun?'

'Yes. Without permission.'

Winthrop dropped the grass and turned toward Fessler. 'What permission? He's a civilian.'

'But he's in the employ of the Army, Albert. He can't just get on his horse and ride off.' Lieutenant Fessler paused, then threw up his arms. 'Indians!' he exclaimed, getting to his feet. 'No sense of order, no sense of time…'

Winthrop arose smiling bleakly.

They got the detail astride and struck out

again. For a long while Winthrop rode with a closed face, silent and thoughtful. But eventually he turned toward Fessler and said: 'George, there aren't any Indian *rancherías* any more. If Indians stole the cattle, where would they take them?'

Fessler scowled at the ears of his horse. 'How does anyone know why Indians do things? I've been on this post and others like it for nearly eleven years. It's always the same with Indians. They sit down and listen to whatever we say, and they ride off, leaving you wondering if they understood, if they agreed or not. How would I know what they did with those cattle, except that you can bet your spurs that they ate them.'

Winthrop dropped the subject of Indians. He had not realized until now that the post adjutant despised Indians. It surprised him only because he had not encountered this attitude in Fessler before, but he had encountered it many times in other places, among other men.

They had a vast expanse of prairie in front

of them when they turned back. Sergeant Flannery had not once got close to the officers. He only met Lieutenant Winthrop's eyes once; that was when the detail came about to head back to the fort, and nothing passed between them by word of mouth or by glance.

Flannery chewed his tobacco and watched the officers up ahead. When Otto Burck came up and said – 'It's not too bad with summer on the land.' – Flannery looked at him and offered a wooden nod in agreement, then continued to watch the officers.

They reached the post in late afternoon. The officers handed their reins to enlisted men, then strode slowly in the direction of the adjutant's little log building. Flannery went with the others to care for the animals. He helped care for the two spare horses, then went out front to watch the adjutant's hutment, and, when Lieutenant Winthrop eventually emerged, he managed to strike out on an intercepting course. They met not far from the dining hall. Lieutenant Winthrop turned and soberly said: 'Go meet him, Mike.'

Flannery nodded his head. 'I thought that was why you turned back early.'

Winthrop sighed. 'If he's got a hide, don't let him ride in with it. And when you fetch him back, wait until after dark, otherwise Burdette's going to see the pair of you.'

Flannery was agreeable to that. 'Then what?'

'Keep him down by the corrals. I'll come down as soon as I can.'

'Lieutenant?'

'What?'

'Do you know why the adjutant thought it might be a good idea for you to transfer out?'

Winthrop considered the lanky man. 'You've got good hearing, Sergeant. Sure I know. At least I can guess why. And because you hate him, you think he's involved with the cattle thefts.'

Flannery gently shook his head. 'No. Not because I don't like him. I think his damned orderly's up to his neck in it, too.'

Winthrop said: 'Go catch Morning Gun before he decides to ride fast to get here before supper.'

Flannery watched the officer walk away, and turned to head back the way he had come. He had no idea who else in the detail might have seen the distant horseman about the time Winthrop ordered the detail to turn about. He was sure that he and the lieutenant were not the only ones, but at least the others had no reason to attach any great significance to a lone horseman approaching from the direction of the northwesterly mountains. He mounted his animal behind the corrals and left the post by avoiding a direct course across the parade ground. It helped that everyone was cleaning up for mess call. The sentry at the gate looked curious, but Flannery dropped the man a roguish wink as though he were on a whiskey run to the town, and the sentry winked back.

Evening was slow arriving, which was a harbinger of summer's longer days, shorter nights, and warmer weather. Flannery, who had a fresh cud to compensate for the meal he was missing, boosted his horse over into a lope and only glanced back once, when he made a wide sweep of the entire area, searching for the rider he and Lieutenant Winthrop had recognized earlier. Just for a moment he thought he had a glimpse of another horseman northwest from the direction of the fort, but when he looked again, there was no such sign.

Between Flannery and the post there was considerable rolling land. There were also thick stands of creek willows. He kept the horse loping until he could discern the oncoming horseman again. He seemed in no hurry. It worried Flannery for a mile or so that the rider might not be who he thought it was. But any time horsemen ride with other horsemen over the years, they can recognize them by the way they sit a saddle even at considerable distances. It was Morning Gun. Flannery swept down into a deep swale and breasted the far ridge, then halted. Morning

Gun was dead ahead about a mile and a half, and he had seen, and recognized, the raw-boned sergeant. Morning Gun changed course slightly so that they would meet atop the rim. Flannery sighed and swung to the ground to wait.

Dusk was coming. Far out, and also far back, it was no longer possible to make out movement. Flannery squatted, eyeing the oncoming rider. He was not sure in the poor light, but he thought Morning Gun had something behind his saddle.

He was right. When the tall Indian arrived and swung to the ground before greeting Flannery, he began freeing the saddle thongs on both sides of the rear skirt. Flannery led his horse close. When Morning Gun let the bundle drop, Flannery caught the smell and wrinkled his nose as the Indian turned, and smiled.

'I only brought back one half,' he told Flannery. 'The half with the marks on it. It was a big hide, more than a horse wanted to carry, along with a saddle and a rider.'

Morning Gun knelt and unrolled the hide.

Flannery leaned in the settling early dusk, read the brands, and straightened up. 'We got plenty of time,' he informed the Indian. 'Winthrop don't want you on the post until after dark. That's a stinkin' hide, John.'

Morning Gun looked down. 'It wasn't fresh when I dug it up.' He looked at Flannery again. 'I found four of them buried in the same place.' He fished inside his coat and brought forth a soiled scrap of brown paper. 'Names,' he told Flannery, handing over the paper. 'Miners. They bought eleven head. The rustlers took the rest of the cattle on among the other diggings.'

Flannery held the paper up close to read the names, then pocketed it and moved back a short distance. Green hides had an aroma all their own, particularly when they'd been disinterred and carried on horseback under a hot sun for a few days.

Morning Gun delved in a saddle pocket for jerky. He offered Sergeant Flannery several curled, lint-encrusted sticks, and Flannery shook his head He was hungry, at least he had been, but right now he had no appetite at all. Morning Gun began chewing jerky. Once, he stopped chewing long enough to say: 'White men, Mike.'

Flannery told him about the detail Burdette had led southward. Morning Gun chewed and listened, then made a grunt of scorn. 'He's not that green, Mike. Pete's good at readin' sign.' Morning Gun spat out some gristle his teeth could not make a dent in. 'A miner told me those fellers told him they'd bought the cattle from a trail drover who was headin' to Montana with a big drive.'

'He tell the miner anything else?'

'Just talk.'

Flannery glanced at the descending night, then down at the rotting green hide. 'By the time we get back it'll be dark enough.'

Morning Gun was starting to kneel when the gunshot blew the stillness apart. He heard and felt the bullet pass him. He heard it strike flesh with a solid sound, and dropped flat.

80

Sergeant Flannery went down in a heap, arms wind-milling wildly for seconds under the impact.

Morning Gun lunged to grab and hold tightly to the reins of his startled, panicky horse. He managed to keep the animal with him but Sergeant Flannery's animal broke away clean and ran in terror back the way he had come.

Morning Gun twisted to look back in the direction that gunshot had come from, but could see nothing. He lay still, gripping one rawhide rein until he distantly heard a horse running, then he got to his feet and led the horse along as he went over where Mike Flannery was lying.

VI

Flannery was alive but there was not much hope. If he had been closer to the post and the surgeon had been at hand, he might have made it. At least that was Morning Gun's opinion as he knelt. Flannery's eyes were so dark they seemed almost black. His face was rigid in an expression of shock, of disbelief. He did not seem to realize Morning Gun was with him, even when John leaned to ease open the soggy shirt, then made a little hissing sound as his breath went out.

Morning Gun leaned down and spoke. 'Mike? I'm afraid to move you. I'll go to the post for help.'

The stiffness gradually departed and Flannery turned his head to meet the Indian's black gaze. 'I thought … back a mile or so I thought I saw someone. Tell the lieutenant it

83

looked like...'

Morning Gun reached for Flannery's hand and held it gently. He remained in that position, holding the hand, for several minutes, then gently placed the hand at Flannery's side and stood up. There was not a sound; the sky was sending forth pale, pewter light. He went to his horse to swing up, and, after gazing a moment at the green hide, he rolled it, retied it behind the cantle, then swung up.

He rode slowly for a mile, then changed direction just in case that bushwhacker was still around, and rode directly to the post, coming in from the southwest, down near the palisaded wall of the horse area. He left his animal tied outside, scaled the wall, landed lightly in the darkness, and stood a long time studying the little squares of orange lamp glow that showed from most of the hutments. It was his intention to approach Lieutenant Winthrop's quarters. He had no idea that the lieutenant had been fretting down among the corrals for more than an hour, until he started forward, and was seen by a stationary shape, which moved with a fluid motion to intercept Morning Gun near the mule sheds.

Morning Gun stopped stone still as the silhouette came closer, then softly asked him: 'Where's the sergeant?'

Morning Gun answered shortly and evenly: 'Dead. Where we met, someone was out there. I think maybe they meant to shoot me, but I was leaning forward. The bullet hit Mike slanting upward from the guts. It was like butcherin' pigs. Blood everywhere.'

Lieutenant Winthrop seemed to stagger. Morning Gun watched him for a moment, then spoke again. 'We got to get him away from out there. Animals will smell the blood.' Then he also said: 'I got a hide with the brands on it, and I talked to some miners who bought the beef. It was white men.'

Winthrop seemed not to be listening. Finally he said: 'I'll get a horse. Meet me out a ways from the post gate.'

Morning Gun waited until the officer was gone, then returned to the wall and scaled it. His horse was tired and hungry. If there had been a way to get a fresh animal and let this one rest, he would have done it. There was no way. He met the lieutenant, did not wait for him to get close, but turned doggedly in the direction of the dead man.

The moon was high before they got there. Winthrop stepped down and stood like granite, gazing at the dead non-commissioned officer. For him, the fury that had come in the wake of his shock and surprise had to wait. Flannery's killing created a distinct, large problem. For one thing, Flannery was not supposed to be out here. For another thing, if it was learned on the post that he had been shot to death by a bushwhacker, the entire command would be boiling mad. Finally, if one of the other scouts from the post came out here with a detail, they would find the tracks of another rider, someone Flannery had met out here. That, more than anything else, would put the fat into the fire.

Morning Gun was squatting near his horse, chewing jerky and waiting. When the officer finally spoke, Morning Gun stood up.

'We can't take him to the fort. He can be missin' for a day or two, which will cause trouble, but he can't be dead from a bullet. That will cause an investigation and all hell will bust loose.'

Morning Gun spat out a piece of jerky he could not swallow. 'You go back,' he told the officer. 'You're supposed to be on the post. I'll take Mike back into the trees and lash him up there the way the Indians used to do. Lieutenant, what about this hide with the brands on it?'

'When you reach the post, hide it somewhere.'

'It smells bad.'

'Cover it. Hide it and cover it. Morning Gun, they're going to ask you where you've been.'

The tall Indian caught hold of his reins. He was not very concerned about that. 'I went to visit some people I know in the mountains. Old friends. That's all.' Leading his horse over beside the corpse, Morning Gun was gazing solemnly downward when he spoke

87

again. 'Who killed him?'

Albert Winthrop said nothing. He helped the Indian get the body across the seat of Morning Gun's saddle, then stepped away as the Indian began making the body fast.

While his back was to the officer, the Indian asked the same question a second time. 'Who killed him?'

Winthrop was not watching because it made him ill to see Flannery's head hanging down like that. 'I don't know. You saw no one?'

'I heard a horse running, afterward. His horse run off, too, back toward the post.'

Winthrop swore. He would have to find that horse and somehow get him into the post. That might not be too difficult. He hoped it would not be. But something else occurred to him. Had anyone seen Flannery ride out? He would bet a lot of money someone had because it was not possible to leave the post on horseback without at the very least encountering a sentry.

He went to his horse, caught the reins, and

stood in thought until the Indian turned, watched him for a moment, then said: 'Now it's all goin' to come out.'

Winthrop had been thinking the same thing. 'Yes. Be careful what you say when they ask you where you've been. If they ask you about Flannery, you've been off the post a week, you haven't seen him.'

Morning Gun gravely inclined his head, still studying the lieutenant. 'The adjutant's orderly will bawl me out. What about you?'

Winthrop turned toward the Indian. 'I don't honestly know, but one thing is damned clear, Morning Gun. Whatever we do from here on must be done quickly. I wish now I'd walked away when Flannery was going to whip Pete Burdette on that scout southward.'

Morning Gun's expression did not change. 'I think it had to be him, too.'

Winthrop had no intention of going into that, so he felt the girth and turned his horse once before swinging up over the McClellan. 'We'll meet tomorrow. I'll hunt you up when

I think it's safe. Morning Gun, be careful.'

Winthrop had the cold in his face on the ride back, without being aware of it. The sentry at the gate was stamping his feet and blowing on his hands when the lieutenant rode through and responded to the sentry's salute. Dawn was only a couple of hours away.

There was no one in the horse area to care for Winthrop's horse, for which he was thankful because he did not want diversions while he worked and thought, then went over to his quarters to get warm, but not to bed down. He remembered the pinched, leathery face of the sentry at the gate; he had been a friend of Mike Flannery. There would be others like that, mostly among the old hands. Winthrop dug out his cached bottle of single malt whiskey, sat near the little iron stove, and sipped. He was not a drinking man, but tonight he had a need for warmth inside as well as outside.

He thought he probably had one day, at the very most two days, to unravel the affair of the stolen cattle. He was almost certain he knew who had trailed Flannery, then shot him. He thought he knew why that had happened, too, but how to prove it was something altogether different from guessing about it. And there was the fact of the sergeant's absence from the post. Winthrop took another couple of sips and re-hid the bottle, then cocked his chair against the log wall, and closed his eyes. He was not asleep when a light knock rattled across the hutment's door, but the sound startled him, and for a moment he continued to lean there, gazing across the little hot room. The second time knuckles rattled the door, Winthrop arose, ran bent fingers through his hair, and went to the door.

The sentry who had passed him through an hour or so earlier was standing out there, bundled against the cold. He looked steadily at the lieutenant and neither nodded nor spoke. Winthrop opened the door wider and jerked his head.

Heat hit Otto Burck like a wall. He blinked,

then reached to loosen his coat as he turned to watch the officer close the door. Winthrop gazed enquiringly at the enlisted man but Burck said nothing until his coat was open and he had shoved back his hat.

'Sergeant Flannery rode out last night and hasn't come back,' stated Burck.

Winthrop walked toward a little table as he said: 'I'm not the officer of the post tonight, Private Burck.'

The bull-necked man acted as though he had not heard that. 'Then you rode out and come back a little while ago.'

Winthrop stood studying the powerfully built friend of Mike Flannery. He pointed to a chair and Burck ignored the offer to remain standing. 'Lieutenant, something is wrong,' he said, never taking his eyes off Winthrop's face. 'I know there is. I asked Mike about it, and he got mad. You're his friend. I sure don't want him to get into trouble by leavin' the post without permission. There'll be muster in a couple of hours and, if Mike's not back for that … him and Lieutenant Fessler don't like each other. Mike's rank come to him the hard way, Lieutenant.'

The uneven way Otto Burck made his statements reflected his worried concern. Lieutenant Winthrop sat down at the little table, hands clasped atop it, and gazed a long time at the older and heavier man. 'Who else left the post tonight?' he asked, watching Burck's face closely.

'No one that I know of, but I only come on duty after you and Mike rode out. Before that a big recruit named Anderson was on the gate. He told me you two had rode out. He said that was all that left the fort.'

Winthrop frowned with concentration. 'Anderson...?'

'Big farm boy,' stated Burck. 'He came in two weeks ago with the replacements. Started out bein' a troublemaker.'

Winthrop gave up trying to recall a trooper named Anderson and said: 'You were Sergeant Flannery's friend. I've seen the two of you...'

'*Were*, Lieutenant? What do you mean I

93

was his friend?' growled Otto Burck.

The lieutenant gazed at Burck without answering for a while, then arose and paced closer to the stove. Over there, he absently reached to close the damper halfway. He was sweating. 'Private, maybe someone else rode out before you went on gate duty.'

'No, sir. Anderson said there was no one went out or come in.' Burck's face was closed down in a harsh expression. 'Lieutenant, I still am Mike Flannery's friend. Why did you say I was his friend?'

Winthrop had made his decision. He said: 'Sergeant Flannery was ambushed and killed tonight, Private.'

Burck took his eyes slowly off the officer and looked around for the chair. He sat down and with both scarred, big hands hanging between his knees looked steadily at the officer. 'Who killed him?' he asked quietly. 'Why?'

Winthrop returned to the table. Instead of answering Burck's question, he asked one of his own. 'How about the civilians, Private?'

Burck was still too stunned to pick up an

implication so he said: 'What civilians? You mean did a civilian ride out through the gate tonight?'

'Yes.'

Burck's blue eyes were narrowing upon the lieutenant. 'I told you, twice now, only you 'n' Mike rode out.' Then he paused before also saying: 'Not while I was out there. I'll ask Anderson again, but he said no one but you two rode out. What civilian, Lieutenant?'

He knew Private Burck by reputation, and gently shook his head. He did not need Burck to go to Burdette's camp and do to him what he had arrived just in time to prevent Flannery from doing a couple of weeks ago. He side-stepped a direct answer. 'That's what I want to know.'

Burck sat a moment with beads of sweat forming on his weathered countenance, then got heavily to his feet. 'I'll find out,' he said, and approached the door as Winthrop gave him a warning.

'Don't say anything about the things we've been talkin' about, Private. Above all, don't mention that Mike is dead. And don't...'

Otto Burck's big fist wrapped around the latch as though he meant to tear it loose and he glared at the officer when he interrupted to say: 'You better tell me what's wrong, Lieutenant.'

It was not the menace in Burck's face and his attitude that made Lieutenant Winthrop point to the chair Burck had just vacated; it was his desperate need for an ally. 'Sit down,' he said, and this time he waited for Private Burck to obey, then Lieutenant Winthrop began at the beginning and talked for a solid half hour.

When he was finished, the bugler calling the post to life was the only sound for a long time in the little log house. Finally Burck arose and returned to the door. From over there he said: 'All right. I'll find out if anyone else rode out last night ... an' I know who you mean ... Pete Burdette. I'll find that out, too.'

Winthrop stood up tiredly. 'Not with your fists, or you'll spoil everything.'

Burck stood looking at the other man a moment, then pulled open the door and disappeared out into the cold, gray predawn light.

VII

Tiredness made men forget – tiredness and shock and pain. Lieutenant Winthrop had forgotten to look for Sergeant Flannery's horse, and, by the time he remembered, muster had been called and Sergeant Flannery had been put on report for being missing and off the post. But all things did not happen for the worse; although the mount sergeant reported a horse missing, the one assigned to Sergeant Flannery, no one went looking for the animal, and a kind fate helped by not having the horse wandering around outside the fort. In fact, that particular horse was never found. Not by the Army, anyway.

Lieutenant Fessler made a point of encountering Lieutenant Winthrop after the orders for the day had been posted. They met over near the enlisted men's barracks where

Fessler had seen Winthrop talking quietly with an enlisted man the adjutant recognized as Private Burck. The adjutant, who was a fastidious man, something that must have caused him frequent moments of agony during his tour of duty at Fort Laramie, eyed Winthrop with mild disapproval and said – 'Dull razor, Albert?' – and, when Winthrop nodded without speaking, the adjutant spoke again. 'You know how I feel about Sergeant Flannery, but being Absent Without Leave isn't like him. Unless of course he'd been drinking. The Irish are like the Indians, they can't handle their liquor.'

Winthrop gazed steadily at the larger man and said: 'It happens to the best of them, George. General Grant was Absent Without Leave.'

Fessler pondered that, decided it could not be true, and said so.

Winthrop smiled. 'He was sent to a post called Fort Jones, out in California, and never reported.'

Fessler never argued with anyone who disputed him when there was a ring of truth to their words, so he changed the subject. 'What in the devil do you suppose got into Flannery? This time it will mean the loss of his stripes.'

Winthrop was watching two men walking together from the barracks nearby in the direction of the corrals. One was Otto Burck, the other one was a massive, stolid-moving man whose uniform was still very blue. He answered the adjutant in an absent manner, and started to move away. 'I guess time will tell.'

Fessler watched Winthrop for a moment, then turned as his orderly beckoned from over in front of the adjutant's office.

Winthrop reached the mount area moments after Burck and the big replacement got down there. He saw them over near the mule sheds and, as he approached, he heard Burck say: 'I didn't call you a liar, Anderson. I simply said that someone else did ride out last night, while you were on the gate.'

The large man did not look angry, just very large and capable. 'It's the same thing,' he retorted. 'An' in front of those other fellers.'

Lieutenant Winthrop walked up, looking from one man to the other. The mule sheds were where these affairs were normally settled because they were out of sight of most of the other buildings inside the walls. 'What is this about?' he demanded sharply. The big man looked dispassionately back and shrugged mighty shoulders. Winthrop ignored Burck. 'If you have energy to spare,' he told the big recruit, 'there are work details to help you get it out of your system.'

The big man finally spoke in a faintly sullen tone. 'Burck said someone besides you 'n' the sergeant rode out last night while I was on guard duty at the gate. No one did, and that's the same as callin' me a liar, Lieutenant.'

Winthrop glanced at Otto Burck, who had told him not more than a half hour ago that a third rider had indeed left the post by the front gate: Pete Burdette. Otto gazed back with no expression.

Winthrop faced the big man. 'You are Anderson?'

'Yes, sir.'

'Sergeant Flannery rode out.'

'Yes, sir.'

'Then I rode out.'

'Yes, sir.'

'And a civilian rode out between the time Flannery left and the time I rode out.'

Anderson hung fire, then said: 'No, sir. I never left my post and no one rode out except you 'n' Sergeant Flannery.'

Lieutenant Winthrop smiled at the big man. 'You didn't leave your post, not even to pee, Anderson?'

'Well, yes, but that only took maybe five minutes.'

Winthrop continued to smile at the large man. 'If someone wanted to leave by the gate without being challenged, he'd wait. That's what happened. While you went over behind the wash house to pee, a man led his horse out, closed the gate after himself, and, when you returned, he was gone.'

Private Anderson gazed a long time at Lieutenant Winthrop. He had learned several things about Fort Laramie over the past couple of weeks, and self-restraint was one of them. He finally caved in. 'If you say so, Lieutenant, but I sure never saw no one, nor heard no one, and no one come through the gate before I went off duty.'

Winthrop nodded about that. 'And there is a regulation about fighting, even down here, Private Anderson. Violation means ten days' bread and water.'

'Yes, sir. We wasn't fightin'.'

'And you're not going to, are you?'

'No, sir.'

Winthrop jerked his head. The large man saluted and shuffled back the way he had come. Otto Burck wagged his head and told Winthrop about the earlier fight they'd had, then he said: 'But I think I maybe misjudged him a little. He's still green and troublesome, but I think there's hope.'

Winthrop ignored that. 'Where is Morning Gun?'

'Out back in the sun. He wouldn't even go over and eat.'

'Did he tell you where he's been?'

'No, sir. We're friends and all, but only when he wants to be.'

'Are you sure about what you told me an hour ago?'

Burck nodded his head. 'The horse had rolled and it wasn't so easy to make out where he'd been rode or not. But he had. The dirt from rollin' was sticking to the sweaty place where the saddle had sat.' Burck's blue eyes did not blink. 'Maybe a horse could work up a sweat without bein' rode, but a saddle blanket can't. Burdette's was still wet with horse sweat.'

Burck stood eyeing the officer for a moment or two, then made an observation. 'He's goin' out this mornin' and I'd like permission to shag after him.'

Winthrop's interest quickened. 'How do you know he's going out?'

'From over at the shoein' shed I watched him right after he'd eaten. He got busy around his camp, brushed the horse, carried the saddle out back, and tied a ridin' coat behind the cantle.'

Winthrop was tempted to turn, but from the mule sheds he would not have been able to see over where the civilian scouts and hunters had their own little private *ranchería*.

'Lieutenant...?'

Winthrop only knew that Otto Burck was a lifer, a seasoned man on patrol and details. He did not want Burck to get caught shadowing Pete Burdette, so he said: 'No. I'll get Morning Gun to do it.'

Burck protested. 'He's dead on his feet, and besides that you can smell him from two hundred feet away. Lieutenant, I've done more of this kind of skulkin' than you know about. I've been in the Army since the Indian skirmishes.'

'He'll kill you, Burck.'

'Not if he don't see nor hear me he won't, and even then it won't be like bushwhacking someone in the dark. I'll lift his hair if he tries it. Only he won't know I'm within miles of him.'

Winthrop sighed. 'All right. I've just detailed you to ride out and look the loose saddle stock over Burck, be back before *Retreat*.'

Winthrop left the oaken enlisted man standing in shed shade and went in search of Morning Gun. He found him, not quite by smell as Burck had suggested might be possible, but by snoring. Morning Gun was slumped against a hay shock back where he could have been located only by accident, sound asleep. Flies were walking over him with eager anticipation. When Winthrop shook Morning Gun awake, the flies fled in all directions.

The Indian rubbed his eyes and said: 'He's hid in some trees. But we can't leave him there very long. It's hot today.'

Winthrop sank to one knee. 'Where is the hide?'

Morning Gun pointed toward a pile where there were even more flies, and where wheelbarrow tracks led from the stalls out back to the pile. 'Under there. It can't add much to that smell. But we can't leave it there very long, either.' Morning Gun picked hay off his stained and soiled clothing. As the officer explained to him that Flannery's friend, Otto Burck, was now involved with them, Morning Gun said nothing, but when Winthrop had finished the Indian looked up. 'What about the adjutant?'

Winthrop slowly smiled. 'Go up there as you are and report in.'

Morning Gun considered that for a moment before getting to his feet, also smiling. As he walked away, the horde of flies flew busily in his wake.

Winthrop got a horse and rode beyond the walls to look for the horse he fervently hoped he would not find. He made a very wide ride in all directions before returning with the heat beginning to make things, including people, wilt. As he was putting up the horse, Corporal Krause appeared to say that the adjutant wished to see him.

He had found no trace of Flannery's animal, which helped his mood. By the time he reached Lieutenant Fessler's office, except for sweat that made him itch a little, he felt better than he had felt since viewing the dead body of Sergeant Flannery. There was one small window in the rear wall of the adjutant's office. It and the door to the outer office were wide open. When Winthrop appeared, Lieutenant Fessler was standing by the window. He turned, nodded, and without moving from the window he said: 'That damned Indian just reported in. My God … can you smell it? I swear he hasn't touched a bar of soap all year.'

Winthrop was sympathetic. 'When people live out of doors all the time, I guess it doesn't bother them. Where has he been?'

'In the mountains, something about visiting friends and sick relatives. I didn't know he had living relatives. Somewhere I was told he was raised by missionaries and was an orphan.'

Winthrop let that pass. 'That's all he had to say?'

'Yes,' stated the adjutant from over beside the wide-open window. 'I think I convinced him that, whether he thinks so or not, he is under orders just like everyone else on this post.'

Winthrop nodded about that. 'And gave him hell.'

Fessler waved a limp hand. 'No. I just wanted to set him straight about a thing we call responsibility, then get him the hell out of here. It's going to take days to air this place out.'

As he finished speaking, the adjutant eyed his desk but made no effort to leave the window. Instead, he gestured. 'There are the papers you can sign for your transfer. I spoke to Captain Brewster. He said he'd prefer that you stayed, but if you're mind's made up … sign them and leave them with Corporal Krause whenever you have the time. Albert, if you take that damned Indian out on a detail, you'd better find a creek.'

Winthrop picked up the papers and walked out. He did not stop at the orderly's table to sign them. In fact, he did not even look at Corporal Krause. He went to the officers' wash rack to bathe, then he changed his clothing, and the last thing he did was drop the papers from Fessler's desk into the little wooden box he used for kindling wood and fire-starting paper.

He did not know the northwesterly mountains. In his thirteen months on the post he had only once even come close to them. That had been when he had ridden out with the entire command, under Captain Brewster, for one of the Army's infrequent showing-of-the-colors formations. They had gone to the edge of the foothills, and because there was nothing over there that was likely to be impressed by their numbers and weaponry except perhaps some shy elk, they had turned back.

Now, he went over to the rear porch of the small post hospital and leaned in the shade, looking toward those distant, blue-burred heights. He had a hide from the stolen cattle, with the incriminating marks on it; he had a dead non-commissioned officer almost certainly shot from ambush by someone who knew Flannery had suspected the thieves had not been Indians, and who also had reason to fear what Flannery might say on the post; he had the word of Morning Gun that there were more of those cattle up in the mountains, along with a number of miners who had bought the cattle in good faith from men they could very probably identify on sight. Most of all, he could not put off forcing this affair to a head very much longer. Sergeant Flannery deserved an honorable military funeral, and, as Morning Gun had said, the weather was warm. It was very likely going to remain that way, and perhaps get even warmer.

He needed a detail to do what he had in mind. That posed no problem. The post commander was a firm believer in uniformed details making a show of patrolling the area. What he knew he would not get without explaining why he needed it was the post commander's permission to be gone with a detail for a week, and perhaps even longer, and there was no way he could give his reasons without also offering the proof he did not have. Nor was he convinced that if he told his story to the post commander, and got permission to make his reconnaissance in force, that when he returned the people he suspected were involved with the cattle-stealing ring would not have fled. The alternative to doing this correctly was to do it in violation of the Army's regulations. Winthrop leaned on the railing of the little porch along the back of the post dispensary and pondered the probable results of what he was going to do. He was not going to make the Army his career. On the other hand as long as he was in uniform, he was subject to Army disciplinary action, and most probably a dishonorable discharge after serving his time as a prisoner in the stockade. He did not want to remain in uniform, but neither did he want a dishonorable discharge.

A solid set of footsteps on the porch caused him to straighten up from solemn consideration of the far mountains and turn. Private Burck nodded and walked on up, his blouse dark with sweat, his thin-lipped, wide mouth curled in an expression of harsh satisfaction.

VIII

As a lifer, Otto Burck knew when it was, and when it was not, permissible to dispense with the Army's rigid codes of conduct for enlisted men toward officers. This was one of those times when it was permissible, so, as he leaned upon the railing a few feet from Lieutenant Winthrop, and he said: 'He went in a beeline to the drover's camp. I'd say the drover and his two cowboys are fixin' to strike camp. They were loadin' a wagon when Burdette arrived. Him and the drover went out a ways to talk. Burdette's been usin' his hands to talk with ever since I've known him, and, while I couldn't get anywhere nearly close enough to hear what he said, he gestured toward the mountains, toward the fort, then he talked like a Dutch uncle for a long time without usin' his hands at all. When he

115

was finished, the drover brought over a bottle and they sat on the ground for the rest of their palaver. There was one other thing. That drover and his riders haven't been at their camp for about a week, maybe longer.' Burck's blue eyes fixed themselves upon Lieutenant Winthrop. 'They was in the mountains.'

Winthrop met the steady gaze. 'How do you know that?'

'Because one of them cowboys workin' at loadin' their wagon called over to the other cowboy who was near their cookin' ring to fetch a little sack of rocks he'd got from a miner.'

Winthrop leaned on the railing, again studying the hazy mountains. 'Anything else?'

'Not much. I let Burdette head back and lay in the bushes for a half hour more. The drover went over to the wagon, and directly him and his riders busted out laughin' about something. Then I got back to my horse and returned. You said to be here before *Retreat*.'

Lieutenant Winthrop leaned in silence for a long time, then turned his head. 'I'm going into the mountains,' he told the other man. 'Without getting permission from Captain Brewster.' He waited for Burck's reaction, and, when the trooper simply leaned there saying nothing, Winthrop added a little more. 'I thought about taking a detail. The trouble with that is Burdette will see us leave, and maybe so will that drover. I could get around that by leaving after nightfall.'

Burck finally spoke. 'You couldn't do it, Lieutenant. Details don't ride out after nightfall except for emergencies.'

Winthrop smiled at Otto Burck. 'You are right, Private. The only thing left, then, is not to take a regular detail, to take Morning Gun and maybe one or two others.'

Burck continued to look at the officer. 'I guess you know what you're saying, Lieutenant ... court martial at the very least.'

Winthrop nodded his head. 'I'm not going to make a career out of the Army, but, even if I was, Sergeant Flannery deserves better

117

than he's going to get from the Army unless I do something about it. Either way, I'm going to be in trouble.'

Burck sighed. 'You know how long I been in the Army, Lieutenant? Since you was in knee pants. You know how many times I been as high as sergeant, and been busted back to a private trooper? More times than you got fingers on your hands.' Burck paused to expectorate lustily behind the little shaded porch. 'It was goin' to happen the same way with Mike because he couldn't shake off being an idealist. He thought everyone, but especially officers, should be downright honest. I know better. By the time Mike would have known what I know, he'd have been busted back a lot of times, too. But you're right. He was an honest man and deserves a hell of a lot better than the Army's going to give him. Tell you what, Lieutenant. You and me and Rourke could leave in the dark and be two-thirds of the way to those mountains by sunup.'

Winthrop knew Private Rourke the same

way he knew dozens of enlisted men, by name and by sight, and that was all. Rourke was a wide-shouldered sinewy man with very dark hair and eyes. Lieutenant Winthrop did not know it, but Patrick Rourke was the lanky enlisted man who had not even stirred off his bunk during that savage barracks brawl a few days earlier. What Winthrop did know about Rourke was that he was a dry, shrewd, taciturn, very experienced lifer who was in Otto Burck's category.

Winthrop said: 'I'm not even sure you ought to go with me. Rourke doesn't even have your excuse … friendship with Flannery. And you mentioned it … court martial. Rourke would have to be foolish to get involved in this.'

Burck said: 'Maybe he won't want to. You said you'd need a couple of men. I'll go, and I'll leave it up to Pat whether he wants to go as well. And, for your information, he was a friend of Flannery. A good friend. All right if I tell him Mike is dead and how he got killed?'

Winthrop nodded unenthusiastically. He was having some early feelings of guilt. 'You stand to lose more than you can gain, Burck. How much longer before you are discharged and pensioned?'

'A little shy of two years,' replied Burck, straightening up. 'Hell, Lieutenant, if I go to the stockade for two years, I can do that much time standin' on my head.' He grinned. 'I'll go talk to Rourke.'

Winthrop said: 'Are you on the gate to-night?'

'No, sir, but Pat Rourke is.' That amused Otto Burck, so, as he moved away, he was grinning.

The lieutenant crossed to the site where the civilian scouts and hunters had their particular area. It was orderly because the post commander required that, but it was nowhere nearly as orderly as it could have been, and that was no accident. The civilians could be paid off, but that was the worst that could happen, and they knew it. Also, this was the way they showed both independence, and veiled scorn for the Army, mostly for officers.

Burdette was not there, but his pair of saddle horses were, which suggested to Lieutenant Winthrop that Burdette had not left the post. He made a dour guess that Burdette was probably over at the adjutant's office. He and Corporal Krause were friends. Otherwise, there was a squawman named McGuire who could have been a Mexican but who was probably black Irish. There was also a lanky Tennessean named Taylor, who claimed to be a relative of a former President, Zachary Taylor. Winthrop had been out with both McGuire and Taylor, and of the two he preferred the Tennessean who, despite his insistence on a relationship that was doubtful and a slow, languid way of moving and thinking, was a very good man on a scout.

Taylor was sitting in shade doing absolutely nothing. He had watched Lieutenant Winthrop cross the grinder and was ready to smile when the officer walked up to his ramada where horse equipment, even cooking and camp utensils, were scattered in something less than the variety of order Captain Brewster required. The lanky man languidly touched the brim of his old hat and smiled as the lieutenant stepped into ramada shade. He said: 'The sergeant ain't come back yet. There's sure a lot of talk going on about that.'

Winthrop settled on a rickety bench, shaking his head. 'No sign of him yet. There's always talk. I've never seen an Army post where there wasn't talk.'

The Tennessean grinned and bobbed his head about that. It was gospel truth, and that was a fact. 'Burdette said him and Mike come near to lockin' horns a couple weeks back when they was out on a detail with you.'

Winthrop was not going to feed that story, so that Taylor could feed his own gossip mill. 'Mike's always getting someone mad at him,' he replied, and leaned back in pleasant shade, gazing away toward the blurry mountains. 'Morning Gun came back.'

Taylor already knew that. 'So I heard.'

'Said he was visiting relatives and friends

up in the mountains.'

Taylor's languid smile lingered but his pale eyes turned shrewd. 'Naw, Lieutenant. There ain't been no Indians in them mountains since old Red Cloud led 'em north.'

Winthrop leaned comfortably, still peering northwesterly from narrowed eyes. 'They could slip back. They've been doing that for years. Maybe just a few, to hunt and make meat.'

Taylor's smile remained, but was fading now. 'Naw,' he said again. 'There's too many miners and little raggedy-ass settlements up in there now.' Taylor paused, then resumed speaking as he warmed to his subject. 'I ain't been up there in about a year, but all the good valleys been staked out and settled. Indians would starve up there. Them miners been killin' off the game until there's hardly anything left. They'd do the same to Indians, if they found any up there.'

'Any large settlements?' asked Winthrop in a casual manner.

'A couple, Lieutenant. You never been back

in there?'

'No. Just once got to the foothills with a detachment, then we turned back.'

Taylor fished inside a torn, not very clean shirt pocket and withdrew a limp brown plug that he offered. 'Chew?'

Winthrop declined.

As he used a wicked-looking boot knife to carve off a cud, the Tennessean said: 'There's a settlement called Beeville. It's got the best meadow. Maybe twenty miners work the diggings in the mountains around there. They got a few married men at Beeville, with women and kids. Then there's a place called Boston. It's about ten miles as the crow flies north of Beeville. The country around Boston is rugged.'

'Is there a meadow at Boston?'

'Well, not much of a one, and it's got rocky soil. They say there's been more pay dirt taken out around Boston than any other place up there. Then there's the individual diggings. They're up darn' near every creek-bed throughout those mountains, and sometimes those men'll step out from behind a tree and aim a rifle at you.' Taylor chuckled. 'They're almighty leery of strangers. I was told to be careful of them loners. I run across some of them. Lieutenant, I don't think they're scairt someone is goin' to jump their claim. I think most of 'em are as crazy as a pet 'coon from livin' alone in them mountains for so long.'

Winthrop declined a drink from an earthen jug the Tennessean kept in the shade beneath his bench, and wandered back in the direction of the corrals. When he found Morning Gun, the Indian had bathed and changed his clothes. He had even dunked his old hat in a trough and had it sitting atop a post to dry out.

Winthrop sat down to ask Morning Gun about Private Rourke. As always, Morning Gun thought over his answer before offering it. 'He came here from Fort Abraham Lincoln. He was a sergeant over there, it was told by Corporal Krause. He came here with no stripes on his sleeve.'

'Is he a good man?' Winthrop asked.

Morning Gun pondered that for about ten seconds before answering. 'Yes. He's an old hand. He don't waste time and he isn't mean. He don't even say very much, but I've been out with him. Yes, he's a good man.' The black eyes slewed around. 'Why?'

'Because Burck wants to bring him along when you and Burck and I ride out tonight.'

'Where to?'

'Beeville first. Is that where you got the hide?'

'No. I got it north of Beeville on a rocky meadow called Boston. Tonight?'

'Yes. You said we can't keep that hide much longer, and you said Flannery can't be left in his tree much longer.'

Morning Gun leaned on a mule-shed wall, gazing at the ground. 'Rourke would be worth taking along. And Burck.' The black eyes rose to Winthrop's face. 'Without leave, Lieutenant?'

'Yes.'

'They'll shoot you.'

'No they won't. I'm not deserting, just going Absent Without Leave. But they don't even shoot deserters in peacetime.'

For a long time Morning Gun studied the lieutenant's profile, then he said: 'What time tonight?'

'Midnight.'

'You want to bring back the cattle, and, if we can find them, the white men who stole them?'

'Yes. And on our way back Flannery's body,' replied Winthrop, turning slowly to return the Indian's gaze. 'And anyone we can find up there who'll ride back with us as witnesses against the rustlers. And when we come back, I want to be able to point at that damned drover and anyone else who was involved in the rustling ... and in Flannery's killing.'

Morning Gun dropped his gaze to the ground again. 'That's a lot,' he murmured. 'They don't like Indians up there, and maybe soldiers, too. How do we get out the gate?'

'Rourke has guard duty at the gate. We'll

lead a horse along for him.' Winthrop studied the Indian's solemn face, then also said: 'I'd like you along because you know that country and you know where the cattle were sold off and butchered, but even if we fetch back all we are going up there for, Captain Brewster isn't going to congratulate us. He's a book soldier.'

Captain Brewster did not trouble Morning Gun particularly. The worst the captain could do to a civilian scout was fire him off the post. He wagged his head gently. He had to go along for one particular reason. He was the only one who knew where Sergeant Flannery had been hidden in a tree. He said: 'I'll be down here when you're ready.'

Winthrop showed a wintry smile. 'I don't want to get you into trouble any more than I want to get Burck and Rourke into trouble.'

Morning Gun almost smiled at that statement. 'We're all going to be in trouble. Good thing people can't be crucified any more.' He was thinking of the stories with illustrations he had seen during his maturing years at the missionary school. He raised his head so that Winthrop could see the faint smile on his dark face. 'I've been arguin' with myself for a year now about whether to stay where I get fed three times a day, and they feed a horse for me, and pay me in silver money each month, or whether to try to be a blanket Indian. I've never been one. Maybe I can't be one. They don't teach you how to live like an Indian at missionary schools. They tell you how unsanitary and bad it was to be like that. But I'd like to try, once, anyway. Maybe when they fire me from here, I'll go up north and make the attempt. Maybe what we're goin' up there to do will have made the decision for me. I'll be down here when you come, Lieutenant.'

Winthrop arose, dusted his britches, and sauntered back in the direction of his little log hut. At least Morning Gun had something he wanted to do after the sky fell; Albert Winthrop had nothing. He hadn't even thought about what would come after the sky fell. He just told himself he was going to be responsible for the other three – and that he must be crazy to do what he was committed to.

IX

Private Patrick Rourke was either a fatalist, or an individual without nerves. At any rate he was on the gate with his rifle, wearing his Army-issue coat and making his sweep of the post, back and forth at intervals, when the last light went out around the compound. He halted, leaned aside the rifle, dug beneath a layer of clothing for his tobacco plug, and picked off as much lint as he could see in the moonlight, then bit off a cud and cheeked it. If anyone had been watching, they would have assumed Private Rourke was bored, but he was unique in that respect; he never appeared tightly wound. He spat, stood a moment gazing down in the direction of the horse area, then picked up the weapon and walked back across the big, barred log gate. Upon the opposite side, he spat, studied the heavens, which had been showing increasing moonlight over the past week, then he glanced in the direction of the barracks.

A couple of horses squealed down among the corrals; otherwise, the post seemed dead to the world. There had been a time when the overhead catwalk was manned twenty-four hours a day, but it hadn't been since Rourke had been on the post, and in fact for much longer than that. The fort's importance as an outpost of the nation – of civilization for that matter – had reached its peak more than a decade earlier. Since then it had been sliding toward oblivion. In another ten or fifteen years the Army would probably withdraw the soldiers and let the place deteriorate as so many other forts had done, eventually picked to pieces by scavengers who needed doorjambs, windowsills, hinge and gate hardware, and eventually the old logs for firewood.

But tonight the fort was quiet and serene by moonlight, Private Rourke its guardian, until his relief arrived in theory an hour after midnight, except that Rourke and

Burck had arranged for another sentry to take over when Rourke rode away. The other sentry was another of the old lifers on the post, and, while being importuned to replace Rourke, had listened, had agreed, then had gazed at the other two with a look of mild reproof; he thought they were going down to the town and get drunk.

Rourke leaned, chewed, and watched for movement down in the mount area. When he eventually saw it, he spat, sighed, hoisted the rifle, and made another march across to the far side of the gate, then grounded the gun to watch as three shadows leading four horses came up from behind the barracks into clear view over by the post dispensary, coming directly toward him. He had a solemn expression as he watched. A man did not absolutely have to be a fool to do this, but it certainly was one of the qualifications.

Burck came first, nodded, and without speaking handed Rourke the reins to a saddled animal. Morning Gun and the lieutenant were already opening the gate. As

Rourke and Burck watched, the sentry said: 'Hammer will be along in a few minutes. He'll put the bar back up. I wouldn't be surprised if he was over yonder, watching from the shadows.'

Rourke started forward in response to Morning Gun's gesture. 'If he is, he isn't goin' to believe this … an officer goin' out with us.'

They did not make a sound, and once outside Burck pushed the big gate closed before mounting and walking his horse in the wake of the others.

Lieutenant Winthrop wanted to be as close to the foothills as possible before first light. He was not especially concerned about someone up in the mountains seeing them – three men in uniform and an Indian – he just did not want anyone from the fort to be able to see them. Of course, if it came down to it, Captain Brewster could put Burdette, or one of the other scouts on their trail. Ordinarily he would not do that, Winthrop told himself. He'd swear and fume and get red in the face, then get busy with the paperwork that would start the wheels of a court martial turning. Captain Brewster rarely rode out any more. Lieutenant Fessler would, if ordered to lead a detachment after the 'deserters,' but George Fessler was not and never had been someone who willingly traded his office, coffee, and stove warmth for riding out.

Lieutenant Winthrop pushed right along. Morning Gun rode with him and said nothing until they had been out several hours, then he simply reined down to a walk. The soldiers could do as they wished.

They, too, slacked off. It was possible to make out mountains dead ahead by then anyway. They would not quite reach the foothills by dawn, but they would be so far away that no one would be able to see them from the fort, not even with Captain Brewster's brass spyglass from the catwalk. There was almost no conversation. They knew where they were going, and why. Beyond that, each of them had his private thoughts to live with.

Patrick Rourke's thoughts had to do with

the stunning shock he had felt when Burck had explained about the murder of Sergeant Flannery, where the bushwhacking had occurred, and Burck's personal conviction about why it had happened. Rourke, like the majority of the enlisted men, did not care much for the civilian pot-hunters and scouts. He especially did not care for Burdette; his reasons for this dislike were private, and they were strong even before Otto Burck had mentioned that he thought Burdette was probably the skulking son-of-a-bitch who had shot Mike Flannery.

As for the others, they, too, were dwelling within themselves. For the lieutenant and the pair of enlisted men, the end result of what they were dong was in their view immutable, so thinking about it did no good. Winthrop thought about what was ahead, and he was grim in his resolve. Morning Gun alone among the four men viewed what might lie ahead not as the culmination of something, but the beginning. He removed gloves to blow on his hands and turned toward the lieutenant to say: 'We got to angle more northerly if you want to go direct to Boston.'

'We're closer to Beeville. We ought to go up there first, then head for Boston if there's nothing at Beeville.'

Morning Gun tugged the gloves back on and rode with slack reins watching the foothills march down to meet them. Beyond were the rough, forested slopes leading to higher elevations. He had a vague idea that his mother may have lived up here at some time, but because the people at the missionary school either did not know about that, or would not give him the satisfaction of their information, if they had known, Morning Gun could only speculate. As they entered the rolling lower country, he mentioned his idea to Albert Winthrop, then added something to it. 'Most people don't know what it's like not to know anything about your family, your father and mother. It's a bad feelin', Lieutenant, a kind of empty feelin'. Nothin' to hold to or build on.'

Winthrop rode in silence for a while, gazing at the Indian, then he made a prescient comment that surprised Morning Gun. 'Worse for an Indian. Whatever they had before got destroyed, and that left them hanging between two worlds without really belonging to either.'

Morning Gun gazed at the lieutenant, nodded, and rode ahead to begin leading because he was the only one of them who knew which trails to take. Sometimes a person found real depth of understanding where he didn't expect to find it.

They rode against their cantles as the land tipped upward. Morning Gun never looked back or to either side after he cut across a pair of wagon ruts that appeared among the trees from the northeast. This was the winding, bumpy road used by the people up at Beeville on their infrequent trips down out of there. It was a long ride up, and they had covered more miles than horsemen ordinarily covered unless they were in a hurry by the time the sun was climbing across a flawless sky.

It was cool, fragrant, and shadowy in the timber. The farther they traveled, the fewer stumps they encountered. Townspeople and settlers did not go this high to cut winter wood, nor did the people of Beeville have to come down this far because they had thousands of acres of timber around their big meadow. When Morning Gun breasted a gravelly flat ridge where nothing grew but some wind-warped rock pines, he halted, looking dead ahead. The others ranged around him, also looking down across a big grassy meadow where tendrils of breakfast fire smoke hung softly above a number of log houses. To Albert Winthrop, who had never seen one of these hidden mountain settlements before, it was picturesque and peaceful. There were horses and mules grazing on the meadow, along with a few milk cows. There was a narrow, deep, brawling white-water creek running on a kind of dog-leg course from over where most of the houses were, down across the meadow. He sat a long time in silence, and eventually said: 'You can *feel* it, no need to own a clock, no need to worry about what someone is doing in Washington, no need to fight or worry.'

Otto Burck nodded his head without speaking. Patrick Rourke, who had seen these hidden places before, and who had come from Manhattan Island back East, spat, lifted his rein hand, and was ready to ride on down there. He was untouched.

Morning Gun took the ruts down off the ridge. They sashayed back and forth, which was the way people driving wagons preferred to climb up mountains or go down them; it was easier on the livestock.

Morning Gun looked back halfway down and said: 'You better do the talkin', Lieutenant. They most likely haven't had a soldier patrol up here in a long time, and they're goin' to figure that's what we are.' He let that sink in, then said something he had told Winthrop yesterday: 'They don't like Indians. No one in these mountains does.'

Otto Burck spat aside before replying to

that. 'I'd guess they got their reasons, John. Trouble with hide-bound folks who live to themselves in places like this is that they don't know a hell of a lot about how things are now ... not like they was ten, fifteen years ago.'

Morning Gun faced forward, said no more, and led them on along the wagon road, down the slopes, and around the switchbacks until they came up through a thinned stand of trees to the edge of the meadow. Lieutenant Winthrop thought the meadow had to be no less than three, maybe four hundred acres in size. It was many times larger than it had to be for the number of animals grazing on it. He could guess the reason for that. Up here where snow came early, piled high, and remained until late, anyone owning grazing animals had to put up hay to see them through. Not everyone was equipped to grow hay, and even fewer people liked doing it.

They saw a stocky man out with some horses turn and watch their approach. The stocky man suddenly turned and walked very briskly in the direction of the irregularly spaced log houses. Rourke said – 'The fat's in the fire, gents.' – and smiled to himself because that stocky man would have run if he hadn't been conscious that the riders behind him would see him do it.

The cabins were all on one side of the meadow – the north side, which was where the winter sun held longest. There were several geranium beds among the log houses. Winthrop guessed that those would be the residences that housed women. But even the unadorned log houses had a clean, sturdy look. There were several little log barns. Those would have been built by the settlement dwellers who owned the livestock out on the meadow.

Otto Burck looked at the lieutenant with a dry smile. 'Rip van Winkle would feel right at home here, eh, Lieutenant?'

Winthrop nodded, and watched men come forth in response to the information disseminated by the breathless, stocky man. A few women came to stand in open doorways, also soberly watching three men in blue uniforms being led by a tall Indian across their meadow. One thing was clear enough; Morning Gun had probably been correct in guessing those watching people had not been visited by an Army patrol in a long while. In fact, the closer Lieutenant Winthrop got to them, the more it seemed that they had not had any strangers up in here in a while, or, if they had, visitors were so rare that everyone turned out to watch them ride up.

He had his scabbarded carbine – Army issue with a trap door and a hammer twice as large as was necessary – and his holstered sidearm. His companions also had sidearms and carbines. Morning Gun was the only one of them who had a lever-action Winchester. As they neared the dusty, grassless place where those miners were standing, Lieutenant Winthrop urged his horse out ahead and raised his right hand. One or two of the miners returned his salute, but most of them simply stood like statues until Winthrop reined up and gave his name and rank, and pulled off his gloves, waiting to be invited to dismount. A large, brawny man with a chestnut beard and a great mass of unshorn hair of the same color made a little gesture. 'Get down, gents. If you're of a mind to stay a spell, there's corrals out back. My name is Amos Bonnifield ... from Kentucky.'

They dismounted, and several of the men turned impassive, weathered faces toward John Morning Gun, who seemed not to notice this. Amos Bonnifield pointed in the direction of the corrals, then began to lead the way. The other men, six in number, were joined by a seventh man, younger than the others, and trooped in Bonnifield's wake like downy ducklings following a mother duck. Lieutenant Winthrop saw Rourke and Burck exchange a look from the corner of his eye.

Out back, when they were off-saddling to turn their horses into a large peeled-pole corral, Amos Bonnifield waited until Lieutenant Winthrop had turned his horse loose, then leaned on the corral beside the officer, gazing from perpetually squinted eyes at the horses as they got down to roll forth and back in hot dust to get the itch out of their backs. He said – 'We don't get soldiers up here very often, Mister Winthrop.' – then he made a sardonic smile. 'Last time I saw a lot of soldiers was about the time of Appomattox.' The sardonic smile lingered and the squinted, steel-blue eyes rested upon Winthrop's face. 'I wasn't wearin' blue, Lieutenant.'

Winthroop smiled back. 'That was a long time ago, Mister Bonnifield. I had two uncles who didn't wear blue, either ... but my father did.'

With the ice broken – comfortably, Albert Winthrop hoped – he said: 'I'm looking for some cattle and the men who drove them up through here a while back.'

'How long ago, Lieutenant?'

'About three, four weeks back, Mister Bonnifield. Mostly, I would like to find the men who drove them.'

Bonnifield's narrowed eyes did not move. 'When I saw you ridin' across the meadow, I figured it might be something like this.' Bonnifield straightened up off the coral poles and turned. 'You gents most likely wouldn't object to some cold buttermilk.' Again Winthrop saw Rourke and Burck exchange a look, but this time the look was easy to decipher. Rourke and Burck were not dedicated buttermilk drinkers. They had been hoping the man with the chestnut beard might have mentioned something a little more fortifying for men who had been in the saddle since the middle of the previous night.

X

Amos Bonnifield led the way toward the front of a large log house, and called for someone named Kate to fetch a pitcher of buttermilk and cups, then he led the way to a large old wooden table beneath a cotton-wood tree, and gestured for the men to be seated. Other settlement men lingered, some leaning, some at the big old table, and some content to squat on the ground in cotton-wood shade. Morning Gun remained standing. Even after the buttermilk arrived and he was offered a cup, he did not approach the table.

Amos Bonnifield was one of those individuals whose style of life had little to do with the passage of time. He stoked and lighted a pipe, got up a fair head of smoke, then sipped his buttermilk before he said: 'About those cattle, Lieutenant. We bought some steers and butchered them.' Bonnifield's habitually squinted eyes were fixed on Albert Winthrop, and, when the officer asked what had become of the hides, Bonnifield gave a forthright reply. 'We tanned 'em. Livin' as we do, Lieutenant, we make use of just about everything.'

Winthrop smiled, mentioned how much he enjoyed the buttermilk, then said: 'Could I see one of those tanned hides?'

Bonnifield nodded but made no move to leave the table. 'You want to see the mark, is that it?'

'That's it,' concurred the officer.

'Was those cattle stolen, Lieutenant?'

'Yes. From the Fort Laramie holding ground, Mister Bonnifield.'

That younger man, the last one to join the others when the detail had arrived, got lazily to his feet and turned to walk without haste in the direction of the corrals behind the house they were all sitting in front of. Morning Gun's black gaze followed the younger

148

man as Amos Bonnifield finally shoved up to his feet, saying he had one of the tanned hides and would fetch it.

During his absence a long-faced thin man with hound-dog eyes and a scraggly beard asked the lieutenant how he had known the drovers had brought the cattle to Beeville. Winthrop's answer was not quite the truth, but it could have been. 'By tracking them,' he said, and the thin man subsided. Around him in the shade the other settlement dwellers looked solemn and thoughtful.

When Bonnifield returned carrying a large cowhide that had been tanned with the hair off, and had a golden supple texture to it, which meant that among the people of Beeville someone was probably a professional at tanning, the same woman who had brought the buttermilk was with him, and, although Albert Winthrop had glanced at her before, this time, when she helped Amos Bonnifield spread the hide on the table, he looked longer. She had the same chestnut-colored hair as Amos Bonnifield, and she was sturdy, muscular, with a golden tone to her skin. She raised startlingly blue eyes to meet the lieutenant's gaze, and slowly smiled. When he smiled back, she looked elsewhere.

Private Rourke leaned with a big hand and traced out the two brands, one a road brand, the other a rancher's mark, then he settled back on the bench in silence and slowly lifted his cup of buttermilk.

Bonnifield watched the soldiers' faces, and read in them what he thought he might see there. He straightened back with a sigh. 'Right brand, Lieutenant?'

Winthrop nodded, raising his eyes from the hide to the big bearded man. 'I'm afraid so, Mister Bonnifield.'

A raw-boned, graying man with a hooked nose and twinkling eyes said: 'Well, Lieutenant, you're goin' to have to use a stomach pump to get your beef back.'

There was a ripple of quiet laughter. Winthrop was smiling when he looked at the handsome girl. She was barely smiling, and was watching him. He shoved back his hat, then gave his head a rueful little wag. 'It's not a few steers, gents. We'd like to get the cattle back, but maybe it's too late for that. What we'd like…'

He was interrupted by sounds of battle behind the house. One man was swearing, ripping the words out. Everyone arose and faced around. Amos Bonnifield took long strides, heading in the direction of the scuffling sounds. Lieutenant Winthrop was directly behind him. Farther back, Patrick Rourke and Otto Burck were among the other men. The moment Bonnifield saw the struggling men on the ground near a saddle horse tied to the outside stringers of the corral, he roared like a bear and lumbered ahead. Albert Winthrop had one clear sighting before the big bearded man obscured the view. John Morning Gun was rolling atop that young man who had walked away some time earlier. Morning Gun had a brown fist cocked when Bonnifield caught his arm from behind and whirled him off the younger man.

Bonnifield was an individual of great

strength, and right now his beard seemed to bristle. He was furious. The other settlement men ran over to assist the younger man to his feet, then one of them, a short, massive man, lowered his head like a bull and started toward Morning Gun. Otto Burck, who had the same build but was taller and larger, had no difficulty intervening. He caught the shorter man by the back and with a grunt heaved him sideways. The short man went down, dust flew; he rolled over and got up onto his knees, spitting dirt and glaring.

Albert Winthrop turned on the others. He made no move toward his holstered sidearm when he said: 'That's enough! Settle down!' He turned toward John Morning Gun. 'What happened?'

Morning Gun was dusting himself as he replied. 'He come out here to saddle up right after you said the cattle was stolen. He was saddling a horse when I asked him what he was doing. He got mad.' Morning Gun straightened around, eyeing the rumpled, battered young settlement man. 'All I

152

wanted to know was where he was going.'

That bull-like short man was on his feet now. He glared and said: 'You damned Indian, it's none of your business what folks do. For two cents I'd...'

Otto Burck pointed a stiff finger at the shorter man. 'You're not going to do anything, so shut up and simmer down.'

Albert Winthrop was looking at the younger man. Morning Gun's implication was clear to all of them. He said: 'Where were you going, mister?'

The younger man stepped back among his friends and turned defiant. 'Anywhere I wanted to go, soldier, it ain't none of your damned business.'

Lieutenant Winthrop glanced at Amos Bonnifield, and in a quiet voice he said: 'I'd like to know.'

Bonnifield, still red in the face, looked menacingly back at Winthrop, but no words came for a while, and, when they did, he spoke to the younger man. 'Answer, Rufe. Where was you going?'

'Up to my claim is all,' muttered the young man sullenly.

'Why didn't you say that?' Bonnifield asked, beginning to look more disgusted than angry.

The younger man's eyes blazed. 'I don't have to tell no damned Indian anything.'

John Morning Gun walked to a stone trough to sluice dirt off his face and hands; he had his back to the others and did not seem to care what was behind him. Patrick Rourke went over there, took down the dipper hanging on a peg nearby, and dipped up some water. Quietly he said: 'Where'd you think he was going, John?'

The tall Indian was using his shirt tail to dry off when he replied. 'To pass the word around the mountains that there was soldiers up here lookin' for cattle thieves.'

Rourke did not drink the water; he instead flung it away and replaced the dipper, then sat down casually upon the edge of the trough, gazing at the rumpled young man. He did not say a word.

Amos Bonnifield said nothing, either, but the look he put upon the younger man spoke for him. He turned on his heel to lead the way back around front. As he passed the younger man, he said: 'You stay here. Unsaddle that horse, turn him in, and stay where I can see you.' As he marched past he said: 'Lieutenant...' Winthrop went with the older man back to the big old table with the hide still atop it. The others remained out back, muttering among themselves.

Bonnifield sat down with a great sigh and said: 'He helped them with the damned cattle when they was comin' up our road. He was at his mine when they went by. They paid him for helpin' them.'

Winthrop remained standing, eyeing the older man and thinking. 'Was he going to warn them, Mister Bonnifield?'

'Most likely, Mister Winthrop. Rufe's ... well, aside from bein' under my feet all the time because he's courtin' my daughter, Rufe's had a little trouble up here now and then.' Bonnifield raised squinted eyes. 'He's been over to the Boston meadow for a few days. That's where your cattle are.'

'Are the drovers with them, Mister Bonnifield?'

'I don't know. I didn't ask Rufe, he never volunteered anything, and mostly we don't go over there very often, got plenty to do around our own settlement. I might as well tell you, Lieutenant, because I've seen the man a few times over the past ten years or so… I don't know his name but he's dark like one of those old French-Canadian trappers who was in this country a long time back. Wears an old scraggy bear-skin coat when it's cold.'

Lieutenant Winthrop did not seem to be breathing when he said: 'What about him, Mister Bonnifield? Was he with the cattle thieves?'

'He come through here on his way up to Boston meadow lookin' for them. Him and Rufe talked, then this dark feller rode north toward Boston. Lieutenant, I've seen him a couple of times down at Laramie, with soldiers. Maybe you know who I'm talking about.'

Winthrop did not say whether he knew the man or not. He said: 'If Rufe was going to ride up there, Mister Bonnifield, it would seem to me he knows the thieves are still up there. Does it seem like that to you?'

Bonnifield turned to watch the men straggling back in the direction of the big old table when he replied. 'I'd say it's likely, Mister Winthrop.'

The lieutenant leaned on the table speaking quietly and quickly, desiring to get something said before all the other men arrived. 'Can you keep Rufe here while I ride up to the Boston settlement, Mister Bonnifield?'

The older man faced forward again and leaned powerful arms atop the table. 'Yes. But for soldiers to go through these mountains without someone seeing them and carrying the word ahead ain't possible.'

Rufe and Morning Gun were with the solemn, silent Beeville man who shuffled back into the shade, and got comfortable

157

there in total silence. Rourke and Burck had cuds they were masticating as they resumed their former places at the table and did not look at anyone. They had thoughtful expressions. Although they were a long way from being greenhorns, they, like everyone else out there at the corrals, had heard enough to have formed suspicions. The atmosphere was strained now. It had never been unguarded, but now it was much more so as Lieutenant Winthrop rummaged for something to say that would be innocuous enough to dispel at least part of the tension.

He had an ally. The handsome big girl with the dark golden chestnut hair came to the doorway of the big cabin and said: 'Father, it'll be on the table in five minutes.' Then she looked directly at the lieutenant and extended an invitation to eat. He accepted for his detail, and with a decent excuse to leave the table arose and jerked his head. All three of his companions walked back to where that stone trough was to wash. Behind them, watching their departure from guarded faces, the settlement men were silent and grim-faced until that bull-like short man growled his thoughts.

'They never come into the mountains they aren't lookin' for trouble. There's no call for soldiers to be here anyway. All we did was buy some cattle and pay cash for 'em.'

No one took up the short man's cause, so he walked stiffly toward a small log house, freshly re-chinked, that had a steep, peaked roof and some large old varmint traps draped from pegs on the front wall.

At the trough Lieutenant Winthrop told his companions what Bonnifield had told him when they had been alone at the table. Morning Gun, rubbing a sore place, spoke cryptically. 'He most likely won't be the only one. I told you they don't like Indians in these settlements. I guess I should have told you they aren't happy toward the Army, either.'

Patrick Rourke finished washing and shook off surplus water before offering his thoughts. 'John might be right, Lieutenant.

Maybe that wasn't the only one who'd try to get up yonder and warn the thieves. I think the answer to that is for us to get up there first. Leave right now.'

Otto Burck was thinking of something else. 'The only person I know who wears a moth-eaten old bear-hide coat is Pete Burdette. Jesus! If he's in it with the others, he's been able to let them know everything that's been goin' on at the fort ... like takin' you on a wild-goose chase, Lieutenant.'

Winthrop had had the same thought back there in tree shade when he and Bonnifield had been talking. At first he had been shocked. Now, the shock was gone. He dried his face and hands, looked at the others, and groaned aloud. He had led them right into the middle of a genuine and dangerous mess.

Morning Gun, sitting relaxed upon the stone trough, said: 'Leave your uniforms here, get some old clothes from these people. Then we leave here about dusk and get up to Boston meadow in the dark.'

Winthrop, Burck, and Rourke turned

slowly to gaze at the tall Indian. He ignored them to sit watching their saddle animals in the corral.

The handsome big girl with the large, robust figure appeared out back and called to them. Rourke and Burck stood transfixed; they had not noticed her before, but they certainly noticed her now. Winthrop smiled and nodded his head, then led his companions toward the house. The sun that was on its downward slide meant less in open country than it meant in timbered country where tree spires cut it off a couple of hours before it happened down where they had come from on the Laramie plains.

XI

The meal consisted of great amounts of heavy food, thick steaks, bowls of boiled potatoes, grainy home-made bread, and more buttermilk. While the men were eating little was said, only afterward, when they all trooped outside, which was customary because smoking or chewing in a house was not considered to be good manners. Out there, the lieutenant sent his three companions out back to look at their saddle stock, then he faced Amos Bonnifield. 'I need your help,' he told the large man. 'We'd like to borrow some old clothes and leave our uniforms here.'

Bonnifield did not look surprised. He stepped to the edge of the porch and perched upon the log railing as he regarded Albert Winthrop. Eventually he said: 'All right.' It was as simple as that, no question, no argument, no surprise. 'I ain't sure it's going to disguise you, what with you fellers riding Army saddles and packin' Army weapons, but all right. You better not wait too long, though. I can keep any eye on Rufe, but I got no idea if someone else from here mightn't have the same idea.'

Winthrop agreed. He left the big older man on his porch and went out back to get his companions. He returned to the house with them by the rear door. Bonnifield and his handsome daughter were laying out clothing. It looked large for the soldiers, but without a word they went into another room and changed. The clothing hung on Albert Winthrop, fit Morning Gun fairly well for length, but otherwise fit him like a cracker sack. Rourke rolled up cuffs and sleeves, but only Otto Burck did not have to do much. He looked at the others, then grinned from ear to ear.

When they returned to the parlor, Amos Bonnifield was not there, but his daughter was, and, whether she wanted to laugh at their appearance or not, she showed nothing in her face when she spoke to the lieutenant. 'Does your scout know the way to Boston?'

Winthrop nodded his head.

She then switched her attention to John Morning Gun. 'Don't take the open trail from here. Go west a mile or so, then parallel the trail.'

John nodded stoically. It had not been his intention to use the marked trail, not after what had happened at the corrals, but he said nothing.

The handsome girl went as far as the back door with them, then stood aside as they trooped toward the corral to rig out their animals, all but Lieutenant Winthrop, who paused in the doorway, looking at her. 'I'd like to thank your paw,' he said.

She brushed that aside. 'He's not here. Lieutenant, be forewarned, the men at Boston settlement aren't like us. If there's trouble, they'll all join in. I've heard it said there are fugitives from the law at Boston.'

Winthrop smiled. 'Thanks for the warning.

With any luck we'll be back tomorrow for our uniforms. We're obliged to you for your hospitality. Is your name Kate?'

She nodded, watching his face; he knew what her name was.

'Kate, when we come back…'

'I'll have some cold buttermilk waiting,' she told him, turned, and went back into the house.

All the way to the corral Lieutenant Winthrop faintly scowled. If she hadn't cut him off, it had certainly sounded as thought she had.

His horse was already rigged out. John Morning Gun swung up and turned northward without speaking or glancing back. He did as the girl had suggested; he left the worn old dusty trail and went westerly through the trees, then, with an Indian's infallible sense of direction, he turned northward again. This ruse was still no guarantee of anything. Someone could have ridden away from Beeville while the soldiers had been eating. But, as the officer told himself, it was better to travel this way than to use the main trail, although it might make it a little difficult if there were ambushers up ahead.

They encountered no one and were kept occupied picking their way around mammoth old deadfalls that a horse could not jump over, as well as stands of trees so closely spaced they had to split up and meet beyond them, and, as they rode, the light down upon the forest floor began softly to fade.

Morning Gun stopped them once, handed his reins to Burck, took his carbine, did not say a word, and walked ahead through the timber. The others dismounted to wait, standing in silence to pick up any sound, leaning on their saddle guns. It was the first time since arriving in the mountains that they were aware of real peril. That scuffling back at Beeville had not been like this at all.

The forest was without a sound. Even the birds were silent, if they were overhead. Rourke and Burck exchanged a guess. 'John didn't like the stillness,' one said, and the

167

other one confirmed this idea. 'It's not natural this time of the evening.'

They were both correct. Lieutenant Winthrop left off listening and turned to watch their horses. At first the animals simply stood patiently, but after about fifteen minutes they threw up their heads, little ears pointing in the direction Morning Gun had taken, and the lieutenant gestured for Rourke and Burck to seek cover. He did the same, then the three of them waited, hands on weapons.

Morning Gun reappeared soundlessly, Winchester in the crook of one arm. When the soldiers walked out, he waved a hand rearward. 'Been a bear up there tearin' bark off the trees for grubs.' He dropped the carbine into its saddle boot and without another word mounted and struck out again, but now he angled more to the west, his idea being simply not to have their saddle animals pass through an area where the rank smell of a bear lingered. Even so, the horses were nervous.

They passed down across a grassy glade,

keeping to the ring of forest on its east side, and pushed on up to the opposite crest. Up there, Morning Gun abruptly halted and sat motionlessly until Otto said: 'Cookin' fire.' Then the scout nodded, and swung off once more, handing Burck his reins. As before he took the Winchester with him. But this time the shadows were firmly settled before he returned. He squatted beside the horse and said: 'There's some cattle on the Boston meadow about a mile and a half ahead.'

Otto had a question. 'What about the smoke?'

Morning Gun, who had been about to mention that, held up one hand with four fingers and this thumb extended. 'Five men at a camp up there.' He lowered the hand and gazed steadily at the lieutenant. 'Pretty dark, hard to make them out.'

Winthrop also had a question. 'Burdette?'

Morning Gun's reply was a little slow coming. 'Maybe. Like I just said, it was hard to make out much more than that there's five of them loafing around the fire. They're cookin' sage hens, and they got a bottle.' He paused, which was his custom. The others waited, their eyes on his face. Morning Gun looked steadily at the lieutenant. 'I know one of them. It's that drover who brought the cattle up to the fort.'

For a long moment no one commented, not until Morning Gun also said: 'The other two are maybe his riders. I guess the others might be men from the Boston settlement. But those cattle are the same kind of stock that was delivered to the post.'

Winthrop was standing at the head of his horse when he spoke. 'How far?'

'Maybe a mile and a half, like I said, Lieutenant.'

'How close can we get?'

Morning Gun was arising to his full height when he replied. 'They're out near the middle of the meadow by a creek. We can't get any closer than the trees on this side until after full dark. Even then, it's a long way to crawl.'

Winthrop gestured. 'Take us as close as

you can,' he said, and stepped up.

From this point on they rode in silent single file, like Indians, being careful about noise. The gloom was thickening. If there was to be a moon tonight, there was no sign of it down where they were riding. Only the smoke scent grew steadily stronger to indicate they were getting closer.

There was a thick, very massive low roll of mountainside to be crossed before they could see the meadow. Morning Gun did not take them up and over it; he instead went eastward until the slope tapered away, then he rode westerly again. The idea of crossing that unforested hill even at night had not appealed to him. He thought they were safe, but after what had occurred at the corral back yonder, he preferred being extremely careful.

Albert Winthrop thought about the man called Rufe, too, and something Bonnifield had said about there perhaps being others back at Beeville who might try to warn the cattle thieves. He had never been in action before. He had been trained for such a condition, but it was not the same. Certainly, under the present circumstances, it was not the same. This time, the Army was going to be outnumbered even if nothing serious happened. He glanced at Otto Burck, then at Patrick Rourke. They were riding with their heads up, eyes moving. Obviously they were not as green as he was at this kind of an affair. Winthrop's lips tightened a little. This was not an Army affair. In fact, if the Army knew where he was and what he was doing, quite possibly it would send a strong detachment after him, which meant that win or lose he had enemies in back as well as in front. If that wasn't enough, he now knew he and his companions were in an area where soldiers were not particularly admired. Finally, if what the handsome big girl with the beautiful hair had said was true, up ahead they were going to face people who were likely to be even more hostile than the settlers had been back at Beeville. He looked again at the pair of enlisted men. They were chewing, peering through the gathering late dusk, and now they had carbines balancing across their laps.

Morning Gun raised a hand, stepped down, and wordlessly went in search of a tree to tie his horse. The others followed his example. When they came forward, the Indian used his Winchester to point with. 'To our right down where the trees end, you'll see their fire.'

With that said, he struck out, and, because this was a forest with the usual clutter of rotting limbs, underbrush, and treacherous footing, he moved slowly, frequently looking back to watch the soldiers. If someone fell or was tripped by a root, it would not be heard out where that fire was, but he did not want it to happen. A sprained ankle or injured knee was nothing they needed at this point.

The fire burned like a red jewel out through the trees, visible a great distance. Upon the far side of it a fair distance, there were other lights, lamps showing through cabin windows. The smell of wood smoke was stronger when Morning Gun finally stopped, leaned upon a shaggy-barked old fir tree, and waited for his companions to finish their study and speak. It was a long wait. Lieutenant Winthrop wagged his head. There was only one way to reach that rustler camp: by crawling through the grass, which was tall enough to provide shelter at night, but during the daylight hours no such attempt would have succeeded.

'At least a mile,' he observed.

Morning Gun said nothing.

Otto Burck spat and turned slightly to study the more distant log houses. 'I don't mind wearin' out the knees of my britches,' he said musingly, 'but I'd hate to get about halfway and have some damned dogs start raising hell when we're too far from here to get back.'

Morning Gun was realistic about that possibility. 'Up in a place like this, dogs bark at something every night. Bears, lions, even skunks and raccoons.' He paused, still watching the distant fire. 'I don't think we can catch them without a fight.' Winthrop turned to look at the Indian's profile. 'If that's the drover and his riders,' murmured Morning Gun, 'we got to make a complete surprise, or there's going to be blood. I've seen those men at the holding ground. They're experienced. They've been up a lot of hard trails.'

Burck jettisoned his cud and met Patrick Rourke's gaze. Burck made a tight little grin. 'You're crazy to be up here,' he said softly, and Rourke agreed with that while resuming his study of the distant fire. 'You're dead right. You're crazy to be up here, too.'

Lieutenant Winthrop had heard little of this exchange; he was speculating about how far across that open meadow they might be able to ride before they would have to start crawling. Patrick Rourke scotched the idea accidentally when he said: 'We couldn't ride out there anyway. No place to tie the horses.'

Morning Gun hoisted his carbine and looked impatiently at the officer. Lieutenant Winthrop said: 'Walk. We won't have to start crawling for a ways yet.'

Morning Gun obeyed, eyes fixed upon the fire. Winthrop was correct. Even though the moon was now rising, and it was fuller than it had been last night, there was one of those typical mountain shades of blackness that seemed not to be limited to the heavily forested uplands; it also spread an aura of sootiness part way across open meadows such as the one Morning Gun was crossing now, with the other men around him. They saw humps to their right, which were bedded cattle. Morning Gun led the way well away from that area so as not to arouse the animals, and they almost walked into another bed ground where cattle had caught either their sound or scent, and were staring, ready to spring up. Some of the animals arose before the danger of two-legged things being close really posed a threat.

Morning Gun waved an arm, then sank to the ground. The others followed his example. They remained flat and still for a long time before Morning Gun left his Winchester in the grass and started to snake-crawl. Lieutenant Winthrop scowled, but kept silent. They watched the Indian until the backgrounding humps of bedded cattle obscured him, then they simply waited. There was no hurry to reach the rustler camp anyway.

Morning Gun came crawling back after a while, and sat up. 'Same brands,' he told Lieutenant Winthrop, and gestured. 'Maybe ten, fifteen head that I could see.'

Winthrop acknowledged this with a dry comment. 'Good thing we got here when we did … the figure missing as I heard it was thirty head.'

As they arose to start forward, the bedded cattle sprang up, but they did not run, they stood poised to though, until even the smell of the two-legged creatures was faint.

XII

They halted when a distant bark of coarse laughter reached them. Lieutenant Winthrop thought they had covered more than half a mile, but in such light the only way he could arrive at any figure at all was by the nearness of the fire. He looked at his companions and Otto Burck grinned, then groaned and got down on all fours. The others said nothing. Now the lieutenant took the lead. He had to stop often, because, although this meadow looked smooth, it had small, sharp rocks all over the upper layer of soil. It was hard on hands and knees.

They had the fire as their beacon. The more distinct it became, the more encouraged they were, and the next blast of laughter sounded clearly. They halted eventually when the lieutenant thought they might be in rifle range.

This time, he put into words what had been forming in his mind since the last halt. 'When I signal,' he told Burck and Rourke, 'you two go west and come down upon them from out there. Morning Gun and I will keep going from the south.' He started crawling again before the others could say anything. Finally it was possible to make out individual outlines. There probably had been five men at the rustler camp when Morning Gun had scouted it earlier, but now by the lieutenant's count there were seven men, and that made him halt again after only a few yards, and turn back to his companions. Patrick Rourke had made the same tally and shook his head at the officer. 'Big odds,' he said, 'even if we surprise them.'

That was true. It was also very possible that, if the rustlers had been drinking, that they would not yield even though they might be caught by surprise. Morning Gun sank low upon the chilly ground. 'We wait,' he announced. 'Those other men must be from the cabins. Maybe out here to drink whiskey with the rustlers.'

There was no alternative, unless they cared to take a long chance. Albert Winthrop sat flat down with his carbine in the grass, and examined his knees. One trouser leg was worn through and the other one would be worn through if they had to crawl much farther.

They got as comfortable as they could, with cold mountain air closing in upon the gravelly valley. The men at the fire were warm, recently fed, and had some whiskey. There was quite a contrast between the two groups. Rourke smacked his lips and Burck grinned. A drink of that whiskey would go a long way right now toward dispelling the cold. Lieutenant Winthrop sat gazing in the direction of the fire, but when he spoke, it was about something that had nothing to do with getting warm.

'I think Bonnifield's daughter doesn't like soldiers,' he said.

Burck and Rourke exchanged a wide-eyed look. Morning Gun, who had been watching the camp, turned his head slowly. None of them spoke until the lieutenant spoke again. 'There is a lot of that, but if it wasn't for the Army out here…'

They waited for him to finish. Instead, he sat perfectly still with his head cocked. It was Morning Gun who said: 'There is a rider comin' from behind us.'

Burck twisted to look back. He had already decided who that would be. 'Someone from Beeville. Likely the one they call Rufe. I hope to hell he didn't see our horses.'

The distant rider was moving at a slow lope. If he had found their animals and had turned them loose to set the soldiers and their scout on foot, they were not in an enviable position. Otto did not think the oncoming rider had found their horses. He told them that without giving his reason for saying it. He was listening. When he spoke again, it was to make a suggestion. 'We can't shoot him, and we sure as hell can't outrun him.'

Lieutenant Winthrop looked toward the fire, then in the direction from which the rider was approaching. It seemed unreasonable to believe the horseman was not heading straight for the fire. If he were indeed from Beeville, abroad this late on a cold night and aiming toward the fire, it was very likely that he had left his settlement to get over here and warn the rustlers about an Army detail being in the area, asking questions about stolen beef. He arose, left his carbine in the grass, and walked back the way they had come to this spot. As he moved past the two enlisted men, he said: 'Cover me. I'll meet him out yonder. If it is someone from Beeville, I'll try to get him before he recognizes me.'

No one moved to go with him, or to speak, but all three men watched him walk out into the ghostly night. The only distraction was the whiskey-inspired noise over at the camp where someone pitched another couple of logs onto the fire, and sparks rose wildly for almost a hundred feet into the air. What made the interception possible was something Lieutenant Winthrop had not even thought about. He saw the rider, finally, saw that his course was straight for the fire, and moved across to intercept the man. He drew his Army issue revolver, held it slightly to the rear, and moved swiftly.

The horse saw Winthrop before the rider did. The horse would have shied but the rider had a strong hand on the reins and swore when the animal would have moved away from Winthrop. They were face to face at about fifty feet when the rider finally let up on berating his horse and looked toward the fire. What he saw was a man standing directly ahead of him, smiling in the star shine. The man raised his left hand and continued to smile as the horseman dropped to a walk and came right on up.

When they were close enough to each other to make out more than a ghostly shadow, the rider drew back to a halt, then leaned on his saddle horn, looking down at the smiling man wearing the outlandish, too large clothing. He did not recognize Lieutenant Winthrop in time. The naked six-gun rose slowly until it was pointing directly at the rider's middle chest.

The rider was flabbergasted and did not move. From the opposite direction came another burst of loud laughter. Evidently the cattle thieves and their guests from the settlement had made quite a dent in their whiskey supply.

Lieutenant Winthrop cocked his weapon and said: 'Get down.'

The rider swung to the earth and stood at the head of his horse, staring. He finally recognized Lieutenant Winthrop, but his mouth still hung slackly. What had completely fooled him had been Winthrop's attire, the one thing Winthrop had forgotten about until this moment when he saw gradual recognition spread over the man's face. He ignored the success of his capture, and why it had been so easily accomplished. He told the rider to disarm himself, and, after that order had been obeyed, Winthrop told the man to lead his horse and walk ahead. Winthrop did not have to tell him when to stop.

The moment he saw the other three men, each one aiming a cocked belt gun at him, the man stopped. Behind him the lieutenant dryly said: 'I guess Amos Bonnifield didn't do a very good job keeping tabs on this son-of-a-bitch.'

They told him where to sit, and Morning Gun took his horse and, without a word, stripped it and turned the animal loose, then stepped over the saddlery in the grass and put up his six-gun as he and the man who had attacked him back at Beeville looked at one another. Private Rourke holstered his weapon as the lieutenant moved closer to face the young man Bonnifield had called Rufe. Not a word was said. The captive appeared to sag against the ground; he seemed sure of his fate. Otto Burck walked behind the prisoner and swung his pistol barrel in a short chopping motion. Afterward he looked at Albert Winthrop and softly said: 'That was too damned close. Did Bonnifield deliberately let him come over here?'

Winthrop turned from the slumped body,

shaking his head. He did not believe Bonnifield would do such a thing, but he did not put it into words.

Over at the fire several men were on their feet now, completely oblivious to the grim affair that had transpired within their hearing. They were all talking loudly at the same time. Two of the men started walking away in the direction of the distant log houses. There were only two lighted windows over there now. As they strode away, one of the cattle rustlers called after them, and the other men at the fire laughed.

Morning Gun turned toward the lieutenant, waiting. Burck and Rourke were also waiting. Winthrop faced the distant campfire and, after a long moment, gestured for the two enlisted men to go around to the west. As they were moving away, Morning Gun leaned over the unconscious man, flung away his six-gun, and stepped over him. He and the lieutenant then went ahead a yard or two before dropping to the ground to crawl.

At the fire a man arose, complaining of the

cold. His back was to the officer and the scout. He had a blanket around his upper body that he carried with him as far as a pile of saddlery carelessly flung down. Over there, he dropped the blanket, knelt, and worked with his back to the men watching from several yards southward in the grass. When he finally arose with a cry of satisfaction and turned back toward his friends at the fire, he was struggling into a moth-eaten old bear-skin coat.

Lieutenant Winthrop lifted out his Colt and held it as he started forward very slowly. Beside him a few feet on his left, John Morning Gun kept abreast. They were protected less by grass now, than by the blinding flames of the renewed fire, which was in the faces of the cattle thieves. The rustlers had lost all their earlier exuberance. They were tired men, as well as being half drunk. One spoke and the others ignored him until his voice lashed out in anger, then someone answered him.

'What difference does it make? Even if one

of 'em was to figure he might make some money ridin' down there and tellin' the Army about us an' their god-damn' cattle, they wouldn't get up no detachment before we could see 'em comin' for ten miles.' This same garrulous voice then posed a question. 'Sam, what's the good of goin' back after the damned wagon anyway?'

The angry man had a strong Southern accent. Burck, Rourke, and Morning Gun recognized it instantly. Only Lieutenant Winthrop did not know the drover.

'I'll tell you why we're goin' back after the rig 'n' the team ... because I'm not about to give them Yankee bastards nothin'. Not even one lousy blanket.'

The voice was thick and slightly hoarse. The other rustlers seemed unwilling to press this dispute and silence settled again. At this moment there was a solid sound a few yards to the west of the camp that even crackling wood did not obscure. The rustlers turned instantly, each one of them reaching for a weapon. Half drunk or not they were as

189

deadly as rattlesnakes.

Lieutenant Winthrop swore in a harsh whisper and raised up onto his haunches, swinging his Colt to bear. Someone out there, either Burck or Rourke, had stumbled over something and had fallen heavily.

Morning Gun raised a hand lightly to the officer's arm. He was as motionless as stone, seemed to be holding his breath. Morning Gun was playing a hunch; he had seen how the outlaws had reacted, but did not expect shooting. There were animals out there, too.

It was a shrewd guess. The man with the pronounced Southern accent subsided with a scornful snort. 'What's the matter with you? A damned cow is out there. You seen 'em when we was makin' camp, didn't you?'

His companions put up their weapons and looked into the fire, too humiliated to speak. The Southerner bore down on them. 'Ain't nobody up here to bother us, for Christ's sake. If they'd been comin', they'd have done it a week or more back. Pete? You still scairt of this place? You hearin' things, too?'

Burdette's broad back, broader inside his old bear-skin coat, was hunched toward the fire. He did not reply.

The Southerner showered scorn on them. 'You act like a bunch of damned redskins. Where is that bottle them boys brought out here?' Someone held a bottle aloft. The Southerner snatched for it. 'You believe that crap about ghosts?' He paused long enough to swallow three times and put the bottle aside as he struggled to catch his breath. 'Green whiskey,' he panted. 'Green as a damned gourd. Pete, that story you told us … look at them boys, they're scairt stiff. Ghosts, for Christ's sake, you idiots, there ain't no such thing as ghosts. Pete, you made that story up, didn't you?'

Burdette did not move but he answered. 'I didn't make it up. I could show you the grave.'

The Southerner scoffed. 'In the dark? Like hell you could.'

'In the dark,' stated Burdette. 'That was a long time ago. There wasn't no settlement

191

up here then. I told you … they didn't call it Boston Meadow then.'

'Yeah,' replied the Southerner, his voice thick with contempt and ridicule. 'Yeah, Pete, you told us, they called it Ghost Meadow back in them days.' The Southerner laughed and tossed the bottle over to Burdette. 'Drink, Pete.' He laughed again. 'Didn't you never hear that ghosts won't have no truck with fellers who been drinking?'

Burdette tipped back his head, then passed the bottle to the man nearest him, on his left. He spat lustily into the glowing fire and looked at the Southerner. 'I buried her not three hunnert yards from this very fire, along with pots and all, then I got on my horse and never stopped again until I was in southern Canada. You want to know why I came back?'

The Southerner had his six-gun in his lap, wiping it when he answered. 'Naw, I don't want to know why you come back. I just want to know that we can get back to the holdin' ground before sunup, hitch up the wagon, and get the hell out of this lousy cold country.' He stopped wiping the gun and raised his face. Red firelight flickered across it. Morning Gun leaned to whisper. 'That is the drover. Are you ready?'

Lieutenant Winthrop did not answer because one of the other men spoke first. 'Hell, what are you talkin' about? We can't get back down to the fort before sunup. Not even if we had wings, we couldn't.'

The Southerner turned on the speaker, gripping his polished six-gun. 'We can, boy, because we got to. Either that, or we set around up here another day, and there's no blessed reason to do that. They paid us for the rest of them cattle, we done collected from off Fessler, give him an' Krause their cut, and now it's time to get on downcountry. You understand me, boy?'

The man who had spoken picked up the bottle instead of replying, and Burdette, who seemed to rock slightly from side to side as he stared into the fire, softly said: 'Buried her not three hunnert yards from here with her best smoked tans on, with her iron pots that she treasured, and I made a little fire and prayed into the smoke, then...'

'Shut up, Burdette,' the Southerner said harshly. 'You an' your god-damned ghost. You made all that up.'

'It's the truth, every word of it.'

'You're lying. All right, what was her name, Pete?'

Burdette answered so softly the name barely reached out where the lieutenant and the scout were listening. 'Her name was Snow Blossom. She was a Crow woman.'

XIII

When Lieutenant Winthrop turned to jerk his head, indicating he was ready to jump the rustlers, he was held motionless by the peculiar look on the face of his companion. Morning Gun was staring at Pete Burdette's back as though incapable of moving his eyes away. His entire body was rigid in the cold night gloom. He remained like that for almost sixty seconds, then very slowly faced the lieutenant without changing expression or speaking. Winthrop softly said: 'Are you all right?'

Morning Gun continued to stare from unblinking eyes and did not answer. Lieutenant Winthrop frowned; he was certain Burck and Rourke were very close by now. He brushed the sleeve of John Morning Gun. 'What is it?'

Finally the Indian let his breath out in a

long, uneven rush, and picked up his carbine from the grass. He was ready, he told Lieutenant Winthrop, in a voice as rattling dry as old cornstalks.

Winthrop looked ahead, then back. He was troubled by the very sudden change in his companion. The reason for his uneasiness was because he did not want to have someone beside him when trouble arrived who for some inexplicable reason could not function properly. He caught Morning Gun by the arm with a gentle shake. 'What is it?'

The Indian was gazing in the direction of the five huddled men at their diminishing fire and shook his head. All he said was: 'We better move.'

Winthrop drew back, still studying his companion, then, as he heard a faint sound from the west, he swore in a whisper and started forward, looking back just once to make certain the tall Indian was with him. He was, pushing his saddle gun through grass and moving without a sound, black eyes fixed upon the lolling cattle thieves.

Lieutenant Winthrop halted within six-gun range, waited for sound off to the west, did not hear anything, and raised his six-gun, looked around at Morning Gun, then cocked the weapon as he called ahead toward the lolling man.

'Not a move! Keep your hands in plain sight!'

It was like jabbing a rattlesnake with a stick. All five of those men seemed to rise from the ground without effort and hurl themselves as far from the firelight as they could, and, as one man landed rolling frantically, he snapped a shot in Winthrop's direction. Two seconds later someone shouted at the man with the gun, then fired twice, very fast. The shooter had been out to the west somewhere, in the eerie darkness. The shooter had hurled himself in that direction before firing toward Lieutenant Winthrop. It was his last earthly mistake.

Gunfire erupted with furious flashes of muzzle blast. Winthrop dropped down and crawled to his right. He heard Morning

Gun's carbine firing with an almost rhythmic series of shots. Rourke shouted from the west, the words indistinguishable, but the meaning clear enough. There were more attackers in that direction. Someone panicked on the far side of the dying fire, sprang up, and fled toward the distant, darkened log houses. For an interval of silence nothing happened, then someone fired a handgun from the northwest, and the runner went down screaming. The noise stopped when other rustlers fired in the direction of that deadly handgun to the northwest.

Lieutenant Winthrop crawled to the east, trying to get around the fire up in that direction, which was where that Texan or whatever he was had been sitting polishing his six-gun and making mean remarks to his companions. Winthrop had already decided the Southerner was one of those people who got disagreeable after drinking. More than that, he had heard every word the Southerner had said, particularly about Lieutenant Fessler and Corporal Krause. He wanted that Southerner alive, and, as he belly-crawled, one of the rustlers bawled at the top of his voice that he'd had enough. What happened next no one ever afterward explained. A hoarse voice answered the cattle thief, telling him to stand up without his gun. Before the man got all the way up, someone shot him. He fell without a sound.

There was so much noise and confusion that what had been an act of deliberate and calculating murder went unnoticed as long as the battle continued. It was not until long afterward that someone from the Boston settlement put it all together, detail by detail, and by then it was too late. The killer was never identified.

Winthrop heard that rustler try to surrender, and he heard a gunshot, but at the same time he saw vague movement up ahead where someone was beginning to push backward to get farther into the darkness, and Winthrop changed his own course to make an interception. The grass was badly trampled near the rustler camp. Winthrop could see the moving silhouette increase its rearward pace, and raised up to aim. Someone yelled a warning, then fired. Winthrop felt roiled air pass his head. He was dropping low when he fired – and missed. But the retreating man had discovered now that someone was after him personally. He rolled over, fired, kept rolling, and fired twice more. He was desperate.

The lieutenant felt a bee sting over his left shoulder, then slippery moisture, but the pain did not last more than a couple of minutes. He rested his gun fist upon his other hand against the ground, and fired. The rustler who had been trying to escape made a guttural roar, raised up, hurled his empty six-gun, and launched himself behind it straight at the lieutenant. Winthrop had one moment to catch sight of a greasy, contorted, brutal face in the moonlight, then the rustler landed on him.

Lieutenant Winthrop clubbed twice with his handgun and missed both times. His attacker was not only desperate, he was wild.

His strength was almost overpowering as he struggled to right himself and lunge for the lieutenant's gun wrist. But Winthrop understood the deadly fury of his opponent, threw the six-gun overhead behind him, and brought the right hand back forward in a fist. He hit his adversary squarely between the eyes, but with only enough power to make the rustler blink, then duck his head to protect his face. Winthrop arched his back with all his strength and dislodged the rustler. Before clawing hands caught his clothing, the lieutenant rolled twice and sprang upright. The rustler was on his haunches, ready to arise when someone yelled from a considerable distance, his voice deep-rolling like a growl of a large bear.

Winthrop moved ahead quickly. The rustler was a thick-shouldered, deep-chested man with a physique that tapered to a small waist and saddle-warped, spindly legs. He threw up a thick arm as Winthrop came in fast, swinging. The rustler raised his head behind the protective arm, small, enraged eyes peering from under thick bone. Winthrop did not let up. His attack was fast, his aim improved as he kept swinging, and, when the rustler finally brought up his other arm and Winthrop hit him hard in the unprotected parts, the rustler snarled a cry of pain, and lunged ahead. The lieutenant swayed aside, aimed his right fist high, hit the rustler slightly behind the ear, and the man with the gorilla physique dropped to both knees, dazed but still dangerous. He wagged his head and turned cautiously to see where Winthrop was – and caught the full force of a hammer blow that dropped him without a sound.

Otto Burck spoke from fifteen feet away. 'Don't shoot him. That's the drover. We need him alive.'

The lieutenant did not have anything to shoot with. He watched Burck walk over, drop to his knees, and systematically truss the unconscious drover using the man's own two belts. Burck went about this without a trace of agitation. When he finished and arose, Lieutenant Winthrop had gone in search of his six-gun. He was walking back, holstering the weapon when Burck eyed him steadily as he said: 'We got two dead ones. This here son-of-a-bitch and Burdette is what's left. But Burdette don't look real good.' Burck cocked his head, then joined the officer in turning northward. There were lighted windows over among the distant log houses, and much closer there was the un-mistakable sound of men approaching. The battle of Boston Meadow had not gone unnoticed.

Patrick Rourke walked up, reloading as he approached. He had a fresh cud and turned aside to expectorate, then dropped the weapon into his holster, and joined the other two in facing toward that sound of ap-proaching settlement men. He said: 'This is goin' to be like walkin' on eggs, Lieutenant. Me and Otto better fade back and stay out of sight in case they're comin' out here loaded for bear.'

Winthrop turned toward the older man. 'Where is John?'

Burck jerked his head. 'Over yonder on the far side of the fire with Burdette. Pete caught one. Lieutenant, that's quite a mob of those settlers.'

Burck was correct. The approaching settlement men were not entirely visible yet, but it was possible to make out that, even walking briskly in a tight formation, there were at least ten or twelve of them, all with star shine reflecting off the weapons in their hands. They were walking right up; the battle was over, there had been no gunfire for ten or fifteen minutes, but, as Albert Winthrop watched them stamping directly toward the dying firelight, his training told him that no Army officer would ever lead men the way those men were being led. He looked around. Burck and Rourke were gone. The bound man at his feet made a choking groan deep in his throat, and feebly struggled. He was coming out of it, but it'd be a while yet.

Lieutenant Winthrop moved toward the fire, but to one side of it, and saw a dead man lying on his face, one leg cocked up over the other leg. He was shocked, but it only lasted a moment.

Among the band of armed men approaching the fire someone called out: 'What the hell's goin' on out here? You there by the fire … who the hell are you?'

Lieutenant Winthrop walked slightly toward the settlers before halting to face them. On his right some distance away he could see John Morning Gun sitting on the ground beside Pete who had been propped up.

The settlement men came up and halted, some with rifles in both hands, some wearing only boots, britches, gun belts, and the visible upper part of their long-handled underwear. Lieutenant Winthrop considered their faces with a feeling of calmness. He told them who he was. He also told them who the rustlers were. He did not elaborate and the silence after he had spoken was not broken until a man with unkempt brown hair pointed to the dead rustler behind Winthrop and said: 'Is he done for?'

Winthrop nodded his head. 'They all are,

but two. Pete Burdette and a man lying over yonder tied with his gunbelt and his britches belt.'

Winthrop's calmness seemed to have an effect upon the angry settlement men. They stood dumbly for a few moments, looking at the wreckage of the camp with its dying fire and its one visible corpse, then several of them walked westward a few yards, and found another dead man. Now the confusion began subtly to change. Two men walked up to Lieutenant Winthrop and glared at him. One spoke harshly. 'You ain't no soldier, not dressed like that. You snuck up here to rob these fellers. Where are your friends?'

Before Winthrop could reply one of the several other settlement men who were over near John Morning Gun, called over. 'This here feller is an Indian.' Their surprise, followed by swift movement away from the light, infected the others. Several voices called out in alarm about Indians. The men facing Lieutenant Winthrop grabbed him and pulled him with them away from the fire, clumsily pushing him ahead as a shield.

A small-boned man with a high forehead and strange, gold-flecked eyes came over to remove Winthrop's holstered Colt. As he did this, he gave the other two men a curt order that they obeyed without hesitation. He said: 'Let go of him. Scatter out. See if those corpses have been robbed.' As the two settlement men moved off, the lithe man gazed at Winthrop with his head slightly to one side. 'You got any idea what happens to renegades who lead Indians against settlements in these mountains, mister?'

Winthrop answered shortly. 'There is one Indian. He was the scout for us.'

'Who is us, mister?' demanded the small man. Winthrop ignored the question. 'Did you buy cattle from these men?'

The lean, lithe man kept his head slightly to one side and did not answer the question. 'I asked you who the other fellers is, who come up here with you, mister. Let me tell you something. In these mountains we got laws and we hang renegades. Now then, for the last time … who was with you?'

'Soldiers,' said the lieutenant.

The lithe man's odd-colored eyes did not waver. 'Where are they, mister? You should have run when your friends did.'

Lieutenant Winthrop answered slowly. 'No one ran, and these men stole cattle from the Fort Laramie holding ground.' He pointed. 'That one lying tied on the ground, bring him over here, and we'll see who is lying.'

'Mister you come up onto our meadow to kill folks, and your friends run off and left you. Where is your horse?'

Winthrop had no chance to reply. Morning Gun called to him. He turned, and the lithe man prodded him with a six-gun. Winthrop looked down, then up at the man's face. For a moment they stared at one another, then Morning Gun called again, so Lieutenant Winthrop turned and started walking toward Morning Gun. The smaller man tracked him with a gun barrel, but did not fire; he instead followed Winthrop.

Pete Burdette was bundled in his old bear-skin coat. His hat had been crushed under his head to make a support. His eyes went to Lieutenant Winthrop's face and remained there as Morning Gun raised one side of the coat. Winthrop leaned to look, then straightened up slowly. Blood was pumping out of a ragged hole in Burdette's thick body. Morning Gun said: 'It hit him from in back, Lieutenant.'

Winthrop sank down in the flattened grass. 'Why did you shoot Sergeant Flannery?' he asked the still, ruddy face whose eyes were still on him.

Burdette did not open his lips.

Winthrop had another question. 'How much money did the drover pay Lieutenant Fessler and Corporal Krause?'

Burdette remained silent, still staring at Albert Winthrop. The settlement man put up his six-gun and leaned down. Softly he said: 'Pete? Who is this feller?'

Burdette finally spoke, but his voice was fading. 'Lieutenant Winthrop from Fort Laramie.'

Winthrop leaned closer. 'Pete … did you bushwhack Sergeant Flannery?'

The fading voice came softly: 'Yes.'

'Why?'

'Because he knew … he knew.'

'And so did Fessler and Krause, didn't they?'

'Yes. Fessler … watched out for us… Fred Krause … kept the accounts … to show the cattle was delivered … and paid for.'

'How long has this been going on?' the lieutenant asked.

'…Four, five years … since they come to the post.'

'Pete, did they know this drover before he brought up the cattle?'

Burdette's eyes wavered, settled upon Morning Gun, and, when next he spoke, it was as though only he and John Morning Gun were there. 'I can't show you … not now … but it's out there. She's out there. I know she is… I came up here now and then … she never spoke to me but there are old-timers around … they saw her … they told me they had … they saw some of the others, too… I told you, John … it was where I wanted to bury her … it was a sacred place … it's always been … a sacred place… I never knew you was alive… John, bury me up here … about a couple hunnert yards straight west of here … will you…?'

Morning Gun nodded gently, sitting in silence.

Lieutenant Winthrop straightened up to his full height looking at the man in the old moth-eaten coat. The slow shock of final realization hit him hard; it was the answer to that odd look he had seen on Morning Gun's face an hour earlier. John Morning Gun had not been an orphan. *Pete Burdette had been his father.* The *voyageur* who had fled with his grief after the death of John's mother, and who had returned many years later as a scout and hunter for the Army. Could he have found out what had happened to his child after all those years? The Indians were gone, scattered among hide-outs in the mountains or on reservations. He might have been able to, if he made a sincere effort to, but he hadn't, and that, Winthrop told himself, was something he may not have wanted to know. Right or wrong, Burdette was going to take that with him.

The lithe settlement man turned as several of his companions came over. Before they could speak, he shook his head and led them away, out of Winthrop's hearing.

John Morning Gun looked up once, and looked down again without making a sound. Lieutenant Winthrop turned to depart and John said: 'He is dead.'

Winthrop knew that.

'I want to bury him here.'

The officer replied quietly. 'Yes. And hide the grave, John.'

'I think I shot him, Lieutenant.'

Winthrop shook his head. 'That wound was made by a six-gun, not a carbine, John.' He turned to walk over where the lithe man and several of his friends were talking. They became silent at his approach. They looked at him from expressionless faces until the lithe man said: 'We didn't know them was stolen cattle, Lieutenant. The last thing we'd have done was buy critters stole off the Army. There hasn't been no soldiers up here since I've been here an' we got no desire to have 'em come up here.'

Lieutenant Winthrop gazed at the smaller man. He was sure of one thing; he had just been lied to. Right at this moment he didn't care. He turned, facing southward, and raised his voice. 'Otto, Pat! Come on up!'

The settlement men turned, as did the fine-boned man with the unusual eyes. So did other settlement men over by the fire where they had placed the dead rustlers face up, side-by-side.

Rourke and Burck did not approach from the south; they appeared in dying firelight from the north, carrying their carbines and looking stonily at the men who were watching them. The lieutenant said: 'One of them was Pete Burdette. He's over yonder with Morning Gun.'

Otto Burck grounded his weapon and

gazed over where the Indian was still sitting on the ground. Then he looked back as he said: 'Is Pete dead?'

Winthrop nodded.

Burck thought about that briefly before also saying: 'What do you want to do now, Lieutenant?'

'Head back to Beeville.'

'Now, in the dark?'

'Yes. Take the prisoners with us, including that one you knocked over the head.'

'The dead ones, too?'

'Yes.'

'Burdette…?'

'No. Morning Gun is going to bury him up here. I'll explain that on the trail.'

Patrick Rourke who had been silently listening up to this point made a protesting statement. 'Lieutenant, we got to wait for daylight. There's no way to drive them cattle through the timber in the dark.'

Lieutenant Winthrop answered that shortly. 'Leave 'em. If the Army wants 'em, they can come up and get them. Lieutenant Fessler and his orderly were ringleaders in the rustling ring. I want to get back to the post.'

Rourke spat aside, looked around into the faces of the men standing like statues, listening, then blew out a gust of breath and hooked the carbine in the crook of his arm and said: 'I'll go bring up our saddle animals.' As he walked away, the lithe man addressed Albert Winthrop.

'Lieutenant, what would you have thought if you come onto someone dressed like you are, out here on our meadow shootin' men?'

Lieutenant Winthrop did not answer; he gazed back over where Morning Gun was sitting motionlessly with the beginnings of a new day paleness outlining him, then went over where the settlement men had brought Rufe, whose hair was matted with blood, and who was sitting on the ground near the fire with his head in his hands, and where the other man who had been knocked senseless was also sitting, his face sickly gray.

The drover did not look up when Lieutenant Winthrop halted in front of him and said: 'Burdette is dead, along with your hired riders. I counted five of you around the fire when we sneaked up behind Burdette. Where is the one who was sitting near Burdette?'

The Southerner lifted his head, forehead creased. 'There wasn't no one sittin' beside Pete,' he said. 'The firelight fooled you. There was Pete, my two cowboys, and me, that was all, after those boys from the settlement left us. Just the four of us.'

Winthrop held the drover's gaze. 'I counted five.'

The drover's reply was vehement. 'Mister, there never was five of us. Not after them fellers from the settlement left. What's wrong with you? There was me an' Pete an' my two riders. That adds up to four.' The drover held up four rigid fingers. 'Four. You think I wouldn't have known if there was someone else up here, settin' near Pete, for Christ's sake? You didn't see no one else ... all right, what did he look like?'

It had been dark everywhere except within the ring of the fire. Winthrop had had fire-

216

light in his face. He had had difficulty seeing any of them, but there had been someone sitting not far from Pete Burdette. Suddenly he remembered something. When Pete had finished drinking from the bottle this drover had handed him, Pete had ignored the silhouette sitting beside him to hand the bottle to a man farther to his left. *Pete had not known anyone had been sitting beside him, either!*

Lieutenant Winthrop stood, gazing into the contorted face of the baffled drover a moment longer, then turned to go over where Otto Burck was talking with several settlement men. When he came up, one of the settlement men, old and grizzled and gray as a badger but with bright, intense pale eyes, smiled and said: 'We didn't mean no harm, mister. It was just that we been visitin' back an' forth with them fellers for a couple of weeks and when all the shootin' started … well, you can see how it would be.' The old man spread his hands, palms downward. 'We bought them cattle fair and square. Ask the drover. He even give us a bill of sale.'

Lieutenant Winthrop watched the old man's lined, wrinkled face without hearing much that the man said. When the words ended, he took the older man gently by the arm and walked out a way with him, then released his arm and turned to ask how long the old man had been up here on the rocky meadow.

The older man laughed a little self-consciously. 'I rendezvoused up here before there was anything. I built the first cabin and made the first sluice box lookin' for gold nuggets.'

Lieutenant Winthrop said: 'Were there Indians around here in those days?'

The old man's smile faded. 'Indians! Yes, sir, mister, there was Indians up here. By God, they liked to scairt me off a dozen times, stealin' my horses, smashin' my sluice with boulders.'

'But they didn't attack you?' asked Lieutenant Winthrop, and the old man rolled his eyes. 'They couldn't do that, mister. Y'see, this here meadow was an ancient burial ground to 'em. They das'n't commit no killin', not even of game, in a sacred place.'

'What did they call this place?'

'Ghost Meadow. Well, mister, in their language it didn't really mean ghost, it meant a spirit, but they're the same, ain't they? Anyway, I never believed that kind of crap no more'n you would.'

Winthrop had one more question. 'You never saw ghosts up here?'

The old man's eyes crinkled in amusement. 'No, and neither did them Indians nor anyone else. That's a lot of hogwash.'

Otto Burck came over to say Pat was returning with their saddle animals.

XIV

The sun was climbing by the time Lieutenant Winthrop's cavalcade rode out of the timber behind the peeled-log corrals of Beeville. They were seen the moment they got clear of the trees. Word spread fast; by the time they had reached the corrals Amos Bonnifield was back there with several settlers.

Not a word was said as the horses carrying the living rustler and his dead companions were tethered in shade. Bonnifield watched Burck and Rourke pull Rufe from the saddle, turn him toward Bonnifield, and give him a rough shove.

The big older man with the chestnut beard glared through a moment of silence, then said: 'Get out of my sight!' Rufe wasted no time in talk; he scuttled away, avoiding the looks of the other settlers. Then Bonnifield

221

walked up where the drover was standing with both arms tied behind him, and said: 'You lied from beginning to end, didn't you?'

The drover looked sullenly at Bonnifield without speaking. The large older man turned his back on the drover and gravely considered the dead men hanging limply over their saddles, belly-down and hatless, then he said to no one in particular that there were no cattle alive worth what they had cost everyone, and turned his perpetually squinted eyes toward the lieutenant. 'Where is your Indian?'

Rourke and Burck, who had been told the story on the ride to Beeville, waited for the officer's reply. All Winthrop told Bonnifield was that they had left Morning Gun back on Boston Meadow to bury Pete Burdette, and the older man's brows shot upward. 'Pete was one of them?'

Winthrop nodded, saw the handsome big girl approaching, and before she got back there, he told Amos Bonnifield that he and his men would like to change back into their uniforms. Bonnifield nodded as his daughter came up beside him, a faint frown on her face. 'Lieutenant, you've been hurt. There's blood on your shoulder.'

Winthrop smiled tiredly. Except for that sharp stinging sensation when the bullet had singed his shoulder, he had not been conscious of the injury. Anyway, it was little more than a scratch; blood always made an injury appear worse than it usually was. He said: 'I'll owe your pa for ruining his shirt.'

She saw no humor in the words and, reaching for his arm, said she would care for the injury, and led him in the direction of the house. Rourke and Burck exchanged a look.

Amos Bonnifield said they should be fed, and helped them care for the animals, and also helped them chain the drover to the corral, then led them over to the house.

Kate was brisk and efficient at cleansing wounds and bandaging them. There were four other women at Beeville; each of them had also been required to learn how to care for injuries. Lieutenant Winthrop sat stripped to the waist as the handsome girl worked on him, as silent as a rock. She finally stepped back to see his face and said: 'You look very tired, Lieutenant.'

He was in fact tired, so he nodded.

She then said: 'And it was a terrible experience.' Again he nodded.

The third time she spoke, she was moving in close again to finish the bandaging. 'I understand your silence, Lieutenant.'

At that incorrect statement he twisted to look up at her. 'I doubt that,' he told her. 'The reason I have nothing to say is because I don't think you like soldiers … or maybe this particular soldier.'

She took a backward step to meet his gaze. 'Why do you think that, Lieutenant?'

'Because the last time we spoke you cut me off and closed the door.'

She regarded him for a moment, then said: 'Lieutenant, I had a beef roast in the oven and I could smell it beginning to burn. That's why I hurried back to the kitchen. And I didn't close the door on you. It's a habit up here because of the flies.'

They remained motionless, looking at one another a moment longer, then she stepped close again and completed tying the bandage as she said: 'I don't know enough about soldiers to like or dislike them … and that also applies to you.' She leaned to wash her hands in a pan of warm water. He watched her thick mane of hair tumble forward, saw the strain put upon her blouse as she leaned, and looked elsewhere only when he heard her father bring Rourke and Burck in through the parlor to change back into their uniforms. She straightened up, drying her hands and looking at him. 'You need rest,' she said briskly. 'I'll hang a blanket over the back bedroom window and you can sleep. I'll see that your men are looked after… Lieutenant?'

'Yes.'

Her eyes moved a little and color rose into her face. 'It would be nice if you'd stay for a few days,' she said, then turned her back on him and became busy at the stove.

Later, when he was bedded down in the

darkened back room, he lay back thinking of all that happened – and the handsome big girl. When he slept, his last conscious thought was of her.

Burck and Rourke declined beds indoors and went back by the corrals to rest in fragrant tree scent. They re-chained the prisoner so that he, too, could lie down if he cared to.

Someone, probably Amos Bonnifield, had covered the dead men with a large old stained tarpaulin and had turned their horses into the corral where they were eating hay.

Otto Burck lay back on soft fir needles. 'Old Brewster's jaw will hang slack when we ride in, Pat. And when he finds out Lieutenant Fessler and his orderly were up to their armpits in that cattle stealin' operation, he'll be fit to be tied.'

Rourke, lying comfortably a couple of yards distant, was more pragmatic. 'The hell with Fessler and Krause, and all the rest. Otto, if we was smart, we'd bury these uniforms and go so far away the Lord himself couldn't find us.'

Burck scowled. 'That's desertion.'

'You dumb Dutchman, what do you think Captain Brewster's goin' to call what we did? Even if he says it's just bein' off the post without permission, that's good for a month in the stockade, then a court martial. Do you like bread and water?'

Burck hitched around until he was lying on his side with his back to Rourke, then he said: 'It's a toss up ... bread and water or the damned buttermilk these folks put into a man every time he sets down.'

Pat Rourke thought about that for a while before he said: 'I wish we'd brought that bottle along those bastards was drinkin' out of around the fire.'

Burck fidgeted irritably. 'It was empty. They'd two bottles, and they was both empty. I looked for 'em. Now shut up and go to sleep.'

'Otto!' exclaimed Rourke as though he had not heard the admonition. 'I always wanted to find me one of those big-built girls with hair like that and...'

'If you don't shut up, I'm goin' to stomp the waddin' out of you. That big girl wouldn't give you the time of day. You seen how she looked at the lieutenant.'

Rourke said no more, but he did not close his eyes for a long time, either. By the time he, too, slept, one of the settlement men came hurriedly to the Bonnifield house to drag Amos out front and raise a rigid arm. 'This time it ain't just two or three, Amos. I've seen 'em ride like that before, an' any time they got one of those little swallowtail flags out front, it means there's an officer along. Look at 'em. There's got to be a whole damned company of 'em.'

Amos stood motionlessly, his narrowed eyes fixed upon the line of soldiers crossing the meadow. His neighbor was right; it was at least a company of soldiers; they had bedrolls and carbines and three pack mules in the drag, while out front was a lanky, slouching civilian, whose bronzed face beneath a disreputable old hat was lean and watchful. The command was not hurrying as it reached the middle of the valley and kept right on coming.

The officer was a few yards behind his scout and in advance of his column. He was a large man, portly, and red-faced as though this kind of thing was something he had not done in a long while.

And it wasn't. In fact for Captain Brewster, whose custom was to relegate undertakings of this nature to his junior officers, it had been a very long, tedious, and tiring ride. In order to reach Beeville, where he had never been before, he'd had to leave a warm bed in pitch dark.

The heat was mounting, too. His outrider was the lanky Tennessean named Taylor. Captain Brewster had wanted Burdette, but the adjutant had said Burdette was off the post. He'd recommended Taylor in his place.

Taylor had been to Beeville a couple of times before, but not recently. He did not have to rely on his memory to find the place; Taylor was a good tracker and Winthrop had left a lot of fresh sign.

Taylor dropped back beside the captain to offer a suggestion. 'I could lope on over there first. Looks like quite a bunch of those miners, Captain.'

The idea irritated Captain Brewster. 'You just stay in point position,' he said, then puckered his eyes to study the gathering of settlers over in front of one of the larger log houses. If the men he wanted were not here, he was going to be more than just disappointed.

Taylor raised a hand when the column was no more than two hundred yards out. The response was not enthusiastic; only a few of the waiting miners returned the salute.

Captain Brewster spoke aside to a sergeant, then pushed his horse ahead, passed the scout, and reached the area of tree shade out front of the log house where there was a large old table. He nodded to the silent men nearby, and swung to the ground, began tugging off his gloves, and ranged a bold gaze over the settlement men, decided the large, impressive individual with the chestnut beard was probably as good a man to address as any of them, and introduced himself. He tucked the gloves under his belt and sat down at the old table. 'I'm looking for an Indian and three soldiers, one is a lieutenant.'

Amos Bonnifield had twice been affronted, once when the portly big officer had dismounted without being invited to, and the second time when the portly officer had sat down at his table, again without an invitation to do so. Amos walked slowly ahead and halted, gazing stonily at his latest guest. 'And what might you be lookin' for those gents for, mister?'

'Captain,' said Brewster, meeting Bonnifield's gaze, 'Captain Brewster. What is your name, sir?'

'Amos Bonnifield, mister. Why do you want those men?'

Brewster reddened. He replied as the column arrived and was dismounted by its sergeant. The men stood with their horses in hot sunlight, watching their officer and the big older man with the thick beard. 'I want

231

them,' stated Captain Brewster, 'for desertion, for stealing government horses and weapons and for abandoning the post.'

Bonnifield thought about that. 'Anything about cattle?' he asked, and saw the portly officer blink. 'Cattle? What are you talking about?' Bonnifield was silent a long time. What he remembered of the Army helped clear his mind; officers relied on adjutants; adjutants were not always reliable. In fact, in the old Confederate Army, adjutants in Amos Bonnifield's experience had not been reliable at all. He said: 'Do you want to talk to your lieutenant, mister?'

Captain Brewster shoved up to his full height. He was not a patient man, unless things were going reasonably well, which they were not at this moment. His face darkened. 'Do you have him here?'

'No, I don't have him, but he is here. Come with me … and, mister, there's not enough room out back at the corrals for all those horses, but at least there is shade.'

He stood waiting. Captain Brewster

turned, barked at his sergeant, then turned back, darker in the face.

The little crowd of settlement men parted for them. Captain Brewster ignored them and went up onto the porch where an immensely handsome large woman was leaning in the doorway. He nodded gallantly as she stepped aside. Inside, the log house was ten degrees cooler than the yard. Bonnifield led him through two sparsely furnished rooms and opened a door, beyond which was near darkness and a man who had been awakened on the bed, struggling to sit up before the sleep had left his mind.

Captain Brewster stepped closer, and stared. Lieutenant Winthrop swung feet to the floor and stood up. He said: 'Captain...'

Brewster felt the presence of the big man in the doorway behind him as he said: 'Lieutenant, you are under arrest.'

Winthrop accepted the announcement without even shifting his eyes. 'All right,' he replied quietly. 'Would you like to hear my side of it?'

Amos Bonnifield dragged in a chair and shoved it forward for Captain Brewster to sit upon. Brewster ignored this indication of courtesy as he replied to the lieutenant: 'When we get back to the post, Lieutenant. I have a full company outside.'

Winthrop smiled a little wanly and sat upon the edge of the bed. 'Not when we get back,' he said. 'Here, Captain.' He began a long recitation. Amos Bonnifield left them alone, but returned a half hour later with two crockery mugs of cool buttermilk. Captain Brewster looked up, accepted one of the cups, thanked his host, but did not raise the cup. He watched Lieutenant Winthrop drain his cup and put it aside. Captain Brewster finally spoke through stiff lips. 'I just can't believe that of Fessler, Lieutenant.'

Amos Bonnifield interrupted. 'Captain, your sergeant is outside jumpin' from foot to foot. He wants to tell you about the dead rustler and the prisoner, I expect.'

Brewster leaned to place his cup gently aside. 'Tell him I'll be along shortly ... and thank you, Mister Bonnifield.' After Amos had departed, the captain arose and paced to the back wall, speaking from over there without turning. 'Fessler, for God's sake. He's an *officer*.' Then he wheeled about. 'Are you sure you can prove it, Lieutenant?'

'Yes, sir. We have the drover. I heard the man say he had paid Fessler and Krause.'

'Burdette, too? He told you he killed Sergeant Flannery?'

'Yes, sir.'

'Jesus! In my command. There will be an investigation. Damn it, Lieutenant, why didn't you come to me the moment you suspected something? Have you any idea what this will do to my record?'

'Captain, if I'd come to you, you wouldn't have listened ... and George Fessler would have found out.'

'Jesus! Lieutenant, I want to get back. When you're dressed, come out back.' Captain Brewster reached the door before he remembered something. 'Where is Morning Gun?'

'He'll be along in a few days, Captain. And, sir, Burck and Rourke and I don't like the idea of the stockade and a court martial.'

Brewster's brows dropped. 'What does that mean, Lieutenant?'

'It means, sir, that in your report you could say that you authorized what we did under cover, because you suspected there was cattle stealing going on.'

Brewster gazed at the younger man for a moment before speaking. 'It would never work, Lieutenant. Army investigators are very experienced.'

'In that case, Captain, I doubt that Rourke and Burck will go back with you. And I certainly won't. Captain, if we've been called deserters, we can't be called anything worse if we really desert.'

Brewster reddened again. 'I told you, I have a full company out there, Lieutenant.'

Winthrop met that threat head on. 'And you'll have a battle on your hands, sir, in which Mister Bonnifield and some of the other settlement men would likely join in, if you take us back under force. A massacre of settlers would look a lot worse than this other thing.'

Brewster's grip on the wooden latch was like steel. 'Nobody threatens me, Lieutenant … did you hear me?'

'Yes, sir.'

'All right, Lieutenant. No charges. My God, I'll crucify Fessler and that damned orderly of his. Are you ready to leave?'

'Yes, sir.'

Out back Rourke and Burck were surrounded by sweaty soldiers. They were enjoying every minute of it. When the two officers appeared, some of their cheerfulness departed, to be replaced with sober looks of uncertainty. Captain Brewster passed orders to his sergeant for the company to be mounted. While this order was being relayed, Winthrop strolled over to Burck and Rourke and told them there would be no charges. They went at once to find their horses and rig them out. Lieutenant Winthrop turned and saw Kate Bonnifield in the rear doorway. He went over to her and smiled. 'Thank you for everything, especially for the bandage.'

She regarded him a trifle pensively. 'You are welcome. Will you ever come up this way again?'

'I'd like very much to, if I was welcome.'

'When, Lieutenant? You'd be welcome.'

'Next week,' he said, smiling a little more assuredly up at her.

'Can you do that?'

'Nothing can keep me from doing it.'

She smiled into his eyes. 'I'll keep watch across the meadow.'

He went back to his saddled horse, swung up, held her eyes until the side of the house cut them off, then took his place up beside Captain Brewster. Far back, with the pack animals, Rourke and Burck rode with their prisoner, and the dead men. Out over the meadow sunlight shone like new gold.

Morning Gun never returned to the fort. Nor did any of the men down there who had known him ever see John Morning Gun again.

The publishers hope that this book has given you enjoyable reading. Large Print Books are especially designed to be as easy to see and hold as possible. If you wish a complete list of our books please ask at your local library or write directly to:

The Golden West Large Print Books
Magna House, Long Preston,
Skipton, North Yorkshire.
BD23 4ND

This Large Print Book, for people
who cannot read normal print,
is published under the auspices of
THE ULVERSCROFT FOUNDATION